acclaim for JACK PULASKI

Jack Pulaski has his turf, and the talent to work it.
(*Andrei Codrescu*)

Get the book and read it. And then shower copies on everyone you know who still enjoys moving his or her eyes from left to right.
(*Sven Birkerts*)

Pulaski has a gift for combining the lyrical with the earthy.
(*N.Y. Times Book Review*)

Jack Pulaski writes convincingly about so many different cultures it is hard to pigeon-hole him. He looks at life through the eyes of Jews, Italians and Puerto Ricans, each change of heart and mind as believable as the one that preceded it.
(*Chicago Tribune*)

The writing is dense, sensual, often hilarious and entirely confident; the characters are real, with sights, sounds, and smells crowding the page.
(*The Seattle Times*)

books by JACK PULASKI

the St. Veronica Gig Stories

Courting Laura Providencia

Chekhov Was A Doctor

a novel by JACK PULASKI

Chekhov Was A Doctor

Zephyr Press

Cover art by Rachel Philp
Book design by *typeslowly*
Printed by Cushing-Malloy

Zephyr Press acknowledges with gratitude the financial support of the Massachusetts Cultural Council and the National Endowment for the Arts.

Library of Congress Cataloging-in-Publication Data

Pulaski, Jack.
Chekhov was a doctor : a novel / by Jack Pulaski.-- 1st ed.
p. cm.
ISBN 0-939010-81-X (alk. paper)
1. Lower East Side (New York, N.Y.)--Fiction. 2. Bronx (New York, N.Y.)--Fiction. 3. Korean War, 1950-1953--Fiction. 4. Russian Americans--Fiction. 5. Jewish families--Fiction. I. Title.
PS3566.U36C48 2005
813'.54--dc22

2004016489

09 08 07 06 05 98765432 FIRST EDITION

ZEPHYR PRESS
50 Kenwood Street
Brookline, MA 02446
www.zephyrpress.org

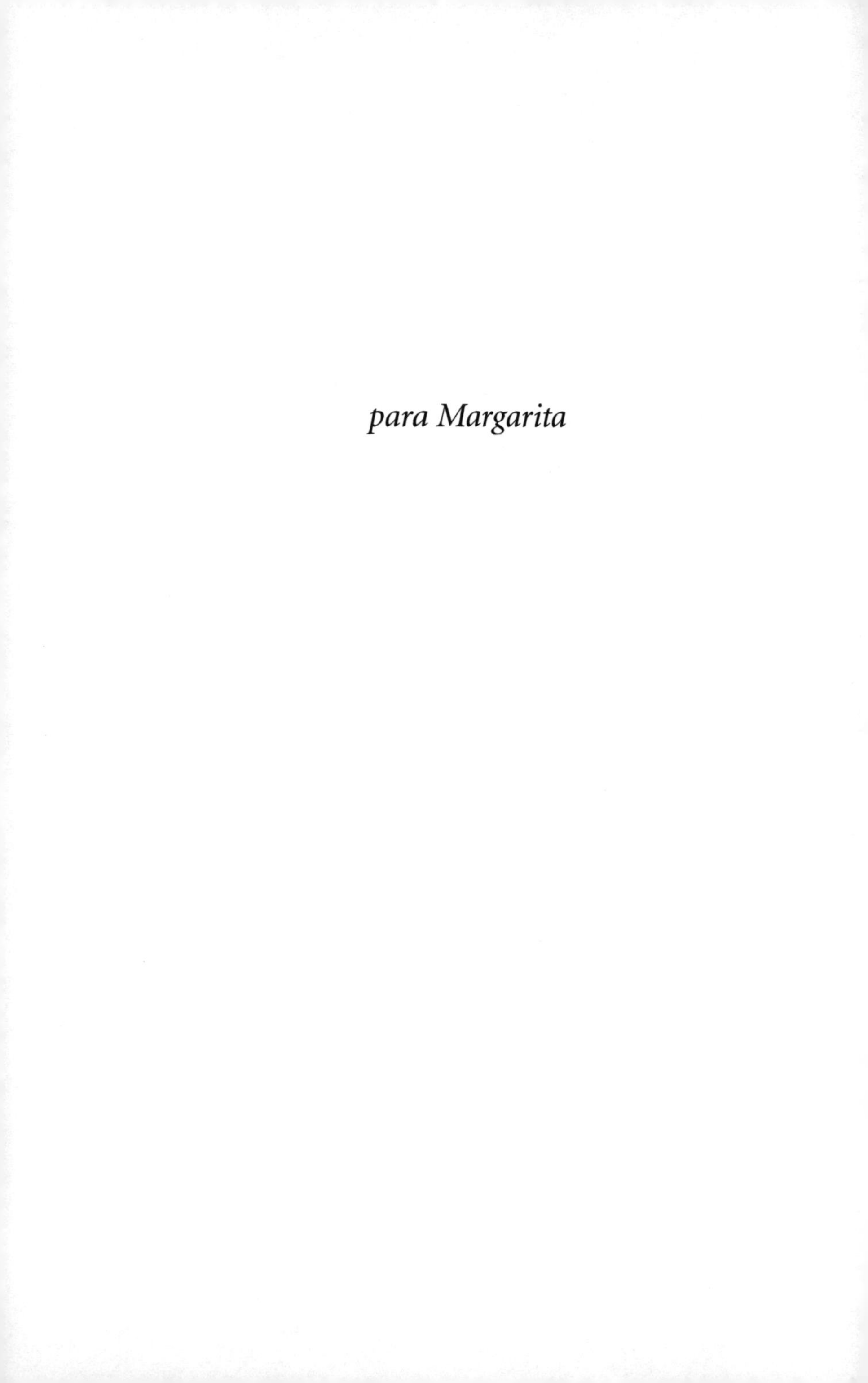

para Margarita

CONTENTS

11 Dialectic
41 Far East
103 La Overtime
183 Saul and Davey

DIALECTIC

THE RABBI HAD BEEN WHISPERING to various family members, attempting to gather what he would need for the eulogy of my father, and Mama said to the young rabbi, "Don't worry about him darling, he's going straight to Hell."

At first Mama thought it was some sort of a trick, because Papa couldn't die, was indestructible, but at last she accepted as a consequence of his delinquency and excess that his combustible heart had suddenly and at last been consumed in a conflagration of his own making and she would never forgive him.

When the rabbi commenced the eulogy Mama shouted commentary and the tribute was turned into the bedlam of Jewish debate, which Rabbi Shein, interrupted time and again, refereed as best he could. The rabbi, making use of the family legends hurriedly whispered in his ear, declared Papa a hero, a defender of the Jews, repeating in astonishment the stories he hadn't time to digest; the rabbi's embarrassment reddened to shame, his enthrallment with the violence an entrapment he couldn't have anticipated as an adept of the oratory which was so much a part of his work; nevertheless, he repeated how Papa as a young man battled anti-Semites in the immigrant streets, relatives all these years keeping score of the numbers of Italian and Irish thugs Papa had sent to the hospital.

"Sure," Mama shouted, tired after a lifetime of awe and baffled by the mystery of where she could be drawing energy from, "Sure, he was a regular one man pogrom, to the Irishes, the Pollocks, but to live with such a hero who rain or shine was a lunatic, that's another story. Go figure, wifely duty, a girl I was when I married him and that horse would ride me half the night, if I let. If I refused him he cried like a baby with colic, for hours and hours, a flood, you couldn't believe such suffering; even me he scared. When I still said no, when I could say no, then he threatened to jump out of the window. He climbed up on the window ledge naked. And sometimes I could still manage 'no.' Then he smashed every stick of furniture in the house except the bed I was lying on; in every street we lived, we were famous."

"But," Uncle Irwin called from the rear of the congregation, his voice plaintive, as if what he was about to say was speculation, not an assertion, perhaps a mitigating circumstance. Uncle Irwin said, "But a provider he was, good times and bad." Uncle Irwin's face was drawn into expert entreaty as he looked at my aunts—mother's sisters surrounding him. "An animal my poor sister was married to," cried Aunt Tessie. The sisters all cried "Animal." "Well," said Uncle Irwin in a hushed tone that suggested that he was only talking to himself, trying to figure out what it all could mean, "A dedicated Socialist he was all his life." "An animal," the sisters screamed. Uncle Irwin turned to me and whispered, "Don't be afraid, this is only normal yelling," and then conceded, "all right, also an animal, but what kind of dialectics is this? I can't figure." The rabbi started to say something about compassion, but mother's scream smashed the words in the rabbi's mouth into a whisper he swallowed. She shrieked, "What I can't imagine is peace. True, I wanted to be a mother, and for this I needed a man, but I had no idea..."

Uncle Irwin tried to salvage decorum and speak his conscience. He exchanged a significant look with the rabbi, as if to say, we are the only reasonable people here; and Uncle Irwin, insinuating contradiction to my mother's sisters, must have felt himself to be committing an act of bravery, puffed up with his oratory. The rabbi and Uncle Irwin blushed, but not for the same reason. Young Rabbi Shein, I thought, wouldn't want to be complicit in Uncle Irwin's presumption of superiority, any more than he'd wanted to be carried away by the legends of my father's epic violence.

Then I remembered another time, perhaps the first time I'd heard Uncle Irwin ask, "What kind of dialectics?" I couldn't have been more than thirteen, fourteen at the most, but sufficiently a man in my father's estimation to be present, there at the Russian baths with my old man's crowd of "Lefties" basting in the pine steam. The scent of pine, the heat, the issues that couldn't be put to rest, present in the chapel as they were in the thick mist of the sweltering Russian room played a trick on every moment there has ever been or ever will be.

Uncle Irwin, medium rare in the bed sheet toga, held forth on the evil of the Stalin-Hitler Pact. I noted the hair that was beginning to sprout on my body. Sitting on the topmost bleacher in billows of steam, large Leo Levitch, built on the scale of what the heroic proletariat is supposed to look like, pulled the damp white sheet around his shoulders and wept. Leo who offered his body, his heart, and soul was incapable of clever argument; nevertheless, as a devout Catholic might feel himself compelled to defend papal infallibility, Leo was compelled to defend the place on earth where the worker's paradise would some day come into being. But as Uncle Irwin hammered at the affinities Stalin shared with Hitler, Leo, veteran of the Battle of the Bulge with a steel plate in his head, couldn't begin to make an answering argument. Russet-pated Leo with the wiry, red hair spawning everywhere but on his head sat, dripping sweat, crying; and I imagined the metal in his head turning to rust. My father sitting next to Leo stood up, wanting to say something to comfort Leo, defend him, but couldn't think of anything to say. Stalin was Papa's kind of guy, the leader whose name derived from steel knew how to cut through clever obscurantist scams. Papa like Uncle Joe had concluded that what he didn't understand was false, a racket, and didn't have the right to exist, and this, I'd surmised, probably included me; moreover, Uncle Joe knew best how to deal with landlords and bosses. That Stalin and many around him were anti-Semites, as Uncle Irwin claimed, Papa answered on another occasion, when digesting a brisket had lulled him toward reason, "Anti-Semites is a condition of being in the world, like the air. First thing is to take care of the bosses and landlords, and when necessary open the heads of the anti-Semites till they learn." He stood there naked, the white sheet having fallen away from his body, and he placed his hand on Leo's shoulder. Looking at my father's powerful body I remembered that I couldn't resist staring at and handling, when no one was looking, Papa's baling hook which rested on the window sill at the end of each long work day. When he put money in my hand for the movies, and I could hardly wait to get to the enchanted dark—grateful for the escape the movies would bring and the unreal stories I wanted so much to be real—I felt, nevertheless, recoil, as if the money I clutched was made of my father's flesh. Papa glistened with sweat, his hand thumped comfort on Leo's shoulder and I saw again, as when Papa bathed in the kitchen bathtub, and I imagined the baling hook writing the wounds in his groin, the livid, herniated mouths that whispered, echoing what the mouth in Papa's head commanded in the kitchen, "Eat, eat," and I complied and knew myself to be a cannibal.

Uncle Irwin wouldn't let go of it. His face bore a peculiar

resemblance to Leon Trotsky; pensive, drooping toward melancholy, it was Trotsky's face grafted on to the face of a basset hound. As he went on and on about the pitfalls of means and ends and the precipitant dangers of expediency, coupling in the same breath the names of Stalin and Hitler, Leo winced and shivered; the ruby globules of perspiration threaded everywhere in the wiry nests of red hair on Leo's massive body, sprayed a faintly pink aureole about him in the pine-scented mist, and he wiped his eyes. Mike, the recently laid off teamster cocooned tight as a giant mummy in his white sheet, stretched out on a dripping stone slab, spoke through a nimbus that seemed to seep from his pearly toes; it grew and drifted, draping his whale-like body. Big Mike defending his pal Leo grunted a diatribe that reverberated in the wet air and was nearly coherent. As I and the others listened to the percussive barking sounds, what became clear was Mike's denunciation and dismissal of Uncle Irwin's moral qualms because, as everyone knew, Irwin was an uxorious husband, "a putz who got down on his hands and knees to wash the floors for his wife." Uncle Irwin speaking as a Marxist protested, saying that washing floors was work too, hard work. Big Mike then said something in Yiddish that exploded laughter from the wet stone walls; the laughter lingered in the drenched air and I pieced together a remark about the meager size of Uncle Irwin's genitals, this judgment annulling Uncle Irwin's analysis of history. And that was the first time I heard Uncle Irwin cry, "What kind of dialectics?"

Big Mike, Uncle Irwin's brother-in-law, claimed intimate

knowledge, and he often reminded Uncle Irwin that he knew Gertie his sister, Irwin's wife, longer than Irwin had. Mike, like a shrouded, beached whale oozing water on some foggy shoal, spouted without any sense that he was divulging something private; what he uttered was evidence because he'd grasped the notion that everything is political and this liberated him for a kind of maximum expressiveness richer than the childhood he'd never had. When Uncle Irwin had made a statement about washing kitchen floors as honorable work a Marxist shouldn't denigrate as woman's work, Big Mike sputtered something—(the glories of erotic possibility connected someway to revolution?) and said, "Yeah, sure, but"—lost the premise that for an instant promised another kind of language, and told how his sister Gertie, Uncle Irwin's wife, had discovered her fourteen-year-old daughter necking with a boy on the living room couch, screamed in disgust "Feh! Throw cold water on them!" and ran for a pail.

We didn't know why we were laughing but it was riotous, aching, echoing in the steaming cave-like Russian room. Doc Sol who was not a doctor but had delivered two babies, one in a kitchen and another on the floor of the garment factory where he worked as a cutter, Doc, savior and paramedic for the neighborhood, well on his way to consuming the contents of numberless libraries, turned to me and said, "I've read that laughter can be a kind of prayer, but not this kind." I stopped laughing. Papa laughing, climbed down the stone bleachers through the clouds of steam. The white sheet in his hand trailed after him. I saw his feral nakedness, whose desire cannot imagine, let alone tolerate impediment without outrage—a tantrum that could leave wreckage in every direction. I knew he was headed for the dormitory locker where he had a bottle. He'd take a stiff belt, groan ecstatically, take another belt, and eyes shining he'd return to the steam room. When we'd first arrived he let me have a swallow. It scorched going down, the flavor of plums smoked through my nose and my eyes teared. I loved it almost immediately. The fluid acuity of everything I saw took on an unimpeachable verisimilitude; but there was more, a hint, a dream of levity, a possibility of freedom that had a wacky religious authority. Papa was doing his fatherly duty before he let me have "a little swallow"; he said, "Davey, you know emotional people shouldn't drink—uh too much," and he looked bewildered; the notion of too much, too much to bear, dissipated in the instant as he anticipated the pleasures of heat. Doc said, "Your father's idea of recreation, like his idea of a day's work, can destroy a person." I attended to what Doc said. He was not only a friend of the family for as long as I could remember, for all practical purposes, Doc Sol was mishpocha, and he was my ally and supported certain of my luftmensch tendencies that alarmed my parents and the other Lefties who were also a kind of kin. Doc looked like a handsome movie version of Abe Lincoln. He seemed always too preoccupied to be aware of his good looks and this only added to his glamour in the neighborhood. Doc, the "Trotskyite" in my old man's bunch, was tolerated and also honored in a begrudging way, (not just for his good works in the neighborhood) but because he was necessary. His midwifery included helping the others say what they wanted to say even when he believed that what they said was folly.

Sitting in the mid-range of heat was Julie Zimmer and he hadn't laughed. Lean Julie's bony frame held the white sheet about him like a triangular tent, the narrow box of his face jammed with all he couldn't say. Julie and his wife Yetta ran the candy store. Yetta short, ample, and voluble compensated for everything in life that had silenced Julie. They'd been married almost a quarter of a century and still held hands.

Yetta at the fountain in the candy store made the creamiest, most sustaining malteds in Brooklyn. The FBI agents who had been assigned to monitor the Zimmers as dangerous subversives, each in turn, became addicted to Yetta's malteds. "Such handsome boys," Yetta said of the agents, appalled by their good looks which seemed to her made of some kind of privileged ignorance; a condition she wouldn't accept as irrevocable any more than she could accept what she called her fourteen-year-old son Ziggy's "stubborn idiocy." Ziggy, an athlete of middling ability, lived in a bland ecstasy composed of his extraordinary capacity for scholarship concerning the performance, potential, physics of movement, diet, and statistics relevant to baseball, football, basketball, and hockey players. Ziggy's imperturbable good cheer was made of his infinite capacity to absorb all, any, and even the most arcane kinds of knowledge regarding athletes who living and dead allowed him to live vicariously through their feats.

What Sidney the Schnorrer had to say about all this plagued the dreams of the Lefties. It lingered after he was no longer around. Sidney the Schnorrer, nearly as adept at theorizing as Doc, had been banished from the group. It was not because Sidney's Marxism absolved him of all generosity until the revolution brought about the classless state and perfect justice, nor his prescient misanthropy that had also annulled desire and ordained his bachelorhood, not even his proprietorship of a pawn shop, but some odor that his soul exuded that only Papa could smell, and the scent caused Papa "to get physical," and so, out of a general civic concern Sidney the Schnorrer had been banished. But before Sidney's banishment he'd said something that continued to haunt, especially, Yetta and Julie.

Sidney's frugality dictated a diet of one meal a day. The one meal was sufficient because of the vanilla malted (which cost a dime including the raw egg whipped into the froth) Yetta made for him. One day, standing at the counter in the narrow candy store, as he wiped the cream from his mustache, he turned from his conversation with Yetta (he'd been enumerating why all reformist efforts to improve the living conditions of working people would fail) and noticed that the young FBI agent, licking the creamy strawberry residue of a malted from his lips, was writing in a pad things he and Yetta had been saying. Sidney, disdaining the existence of the FBI agent as nothing more than an erroneous premise commented to Yetta that the agent and the colleagues who'd preceded him wrote nothing down when Shoot-Him-In-the Leg Facceti's lieutenant, dapper young Marco, came to collect the weekly protection payment that all the neighborhood merchants were obliged to make; but when Yetta had mentioned (and jotted in her little pad) the meeting she and Julie would attend in Spanish Harlem in support of Congressman Vito the Red Marcantonio—who was busy battling the slum lords—then the agent wrote copiously in his pad. Yetta scribbled in her pad; the FBI agent scribbled in his and except for this urgent note-taking Yetta found Agent Shepard courteous, even courtly, handsome in his shirt and tie, and he was always smiling.

Yetta's notebook contained the schedule of meetings, protests, picket lines, imminent strikes where she and Julie would march; the itinerary governed and shaped her husband's life, and granted his gloom moral weight.

Sidney's tongue fished the last creamy drops of vanilla from his moustache and he glanced once more at the FBI agent, who was a visible error in logic. Sidney leaving the candy store sighed, and by way of farewell said to Yetta that it was only the fact of the American masses living vicariously through the performances of professional athletes that kept the country from fascism.

Yetta, who often lectured Agent Shepard on the Triangle Shirtwaist Factory Fire, described vividly girls in flames leaping to their deaths from windows pouring smoke, and the plight of textile workers and miners; Yetta spoke, but was stricken. Sidney was gone. She turned to the amiable sound of Agent Shepard and her son Ziggy chatting. They were discussing the relative merits of Phil Rizzuto the shortstop for the New York Yankees and Pee Wee Reese, shortstop for the Brooklyn Dodgers. Something in the smooth avidity of their speech endowed her sight and she saw for the first time the resemblance between her fourteen-year-old son and the FBI agent. Beyond the fact that they were both blonde (no one else in the family was fair, and the uncanny similarity in the regular features of their faces, to say nothing of Ziggy's snub nose that had to be a genetic mutation) they shared a bland assurance, an obliviousness to the world's suffering that could be confused with grace. Yetta covered her mouth with her hand. She recalled that her husband had long ago looked upon his son as a changeling and retreated into a silence (he spoke only when spoken to and responded with the most perfunctory and sparse speech); Julie's minimal, rarely heard voice was augmented, a little, by the sound of his feet, marching in protest.

On occasion I had played handball with Ziggy. He was an enthusiastic but not a strong player. We played against the wall of the Lovenest Candy Bar factory. There were bricks that jutted out of the wall that made the ball fly at radical angles and that was part of the game. Often before we began play he'd tell me something I didn't know about one of my favorite ball players. I remember when he first mentioned Satchel Paige whom I'd never head of. Satchel Paige pitched in the Negro Leagues and was probably the greatest pitcher in baseball, although because of his color, only got a belated chance in the major leagues. That was perhaps as close as Ziggy had ever come to venturing into the subject of injustice, where his parents lived. Ziggy merely stated the fact. Then he spoke of an older married sister I didn't know existed. I've thought about but am uncertain of what the connection was between Satchel

Paige and the reverie of the older married sister, whose name he said was Betty, and lived far away, in Connecticut. Ziggy too seemed unaware and not in the least inclined to explore and find the connection in his thought that led him to speak of Satchel Paige and the sister no one in the neighborhood, as far as I know, remembered ever seeing. Ziggy spoke of this sister, faraway, with such whimsical longing that at first I wondered whether he was making her up. Maybe this sister had to go away to invent herself. Ziggy said his parents had named his sister after Lenin; her name had been Lenina before she changed it to Betty. Ziggy telling me all this with a contentment just short of joy enumerated droll facts, which included his parents, and Ziggy, like Lenina who had become Betty, would move far away.

I had my own dreams of far away. I'd begun to wander as I closed in on my thirteenth year and Bar Mitzvah. I was having my first argument with God. For the better part of a year my Hebrew teacher Mr. Epstein, who had access to me every day after school except for Friday evening and Saturday, the Sabbath, did his best to prepare me and a dozen other unruly boys for the synagogue ritual of reading from the Torah. All but the most militant atheists in my father's crowd of Lefties made arrangements for the Bar Mitzvah of their sons; perhaps beyond political dogma, the knowledge of the annihilation of European Jewry made the assertion of the Bar Mitzvah necessary.

Mr. Epstein erupted with extemporaneous lectures on Jewish history; his source was the Bible as only that book could provide vindication, while newspapers and radio conveying recent history and contemporary events communicated only what was crushing and unspeakable. Mr. Epstein spoke with a surprising vehemence and as though he'd been there. The only distance Mr. Epstein conveyed was when he lapsed into biblical rhetoric as the truth of what he was saying required heightened language; his breathing was labored as he spoke, his worn, blue-striped worstered suit emitted the dust of a refugee road, and his gaunt face aspired to optimism. Always the stories he told were of escape and vengeance. He told us about Shadrach, Meshach, and Abednego. These three Jews had refused to worship the golden idol that King Nebuchadnezzar of Babylon had made. Mr. Epstein said that Shadrach, Meshach, and Abednego had been appointed to important executive positions by the king and the king was furious at their ingratitude. He commanded the most mighty men in his army to bind Shadrach, Meshach, and Abednego and cast them into the burning furnace. Mr. Epstein clapped his hands and said, "And guess what?" Before we could shout back "What?" he told us the flames had no effect on Shadrach, Meshach, and Abednego but flared and destroyed the soldiers who had placed them in the furnace. I imagined Shadrach, Meshach, and Abednego—devotees of furnace heat—were like my father lolling in an oven until his flesh spouted sufficient water to carry him as close to repose as he would ever get. That nutty Nebuchadnezzar then decreed that any people who spoke against the God of Shadrach, Meshach, and Abednego "Shall be cut in pieces and their houses shall be made a dung hill," didn't strike me as fortuitous and the further troubles in Babylon, Daniel winding up in the den with lions who'd miraculously lost their appetite for Jewish flesh, didn't make a claim on me. But it was the escape from Pharaoh's Egypt that precipitated my first complaint against God's means. Worse than wage slaves, laying bricks when the only compensation was that you could go on breathing to lay more bricks—certainly the Jews had to break out of Egypt. I appreciated the difficulty caused by the Pharaoh's stubbornness. Still, an all-powerful all-knowing and loving God had to have other options than killing all the Egyptian firstborn. All those Egyptian babies were innocent I declaimed to Mr. Epstein. "At midnight," said Mr. Epstein, dazzled by the mysterious muscle of the Jews, Epstein extrapolating how Yahweh, out of patience with hard headed Pharaoh, was through leaning on him, raining frogs and such, now it was Holocaust time, "and it came to pass, that at midnight the Lord smote all the first born in the land of Egypt." Close to my thirteenth year, in the dark, before sleep, in sleep, I harangued God about the injustice.

The dream of the necessary transgression became a nightmare that returned again and again, altered in details, but unchanged in its power to frighten me. I was playing handball against the Wailing Wall in Jerusalem. My opponent was unbeatable and I knew that the one thing I had to achieve was staying power for some purpose that I must take on faith. The lamentations of the rabbis (getting ready to stone me as a disobedient son) were as sincere as my father's remorse when rage overtook him and I could die under his hands, but be brought back long enough to forgive him, because his grief was more than either of us could bear. The ranks of the gray bearded, weeping rabbis shrouded in black gabardine frock coats encircled me, warming up, assuming the postures of baseball pitchers, they were ready to let the stones fly, annihilate me. When I tried to explain that I was playing handball against the Wailing Wall because I needed to develop the necessary stamina, as I couldn't forgo love, and I didn't know whether this was a strength or a weakness, I was only telling part of the truth. The blasphemy I was committing was a transgression that gave impetus to the unknown journey I had to make. I merited punishment and claimed the prerogatives of innocence, since I was, after all, absurdly innocent, like Julie and Yetta Zimmer. What brought the FBI into the candy store, I asked the rabbis rhetorically. Yetta and Julie had been "prematurely anti-fascist" and tried to organize fundraisers for loyalist Spain. Now the Zimmers would be surveilled forever. Was it possible to have an inner life and be surveilled forever? But the rabbis only heard the word Spain and screamed "Inquisition!" From their howling I knew they were accusing me of being a collaborationist, assimilationist, someone willy-nilly in league with those who had prepared the hot lead enemas to bring the Jews to worship the Jew the Gentiles called God.

The dream came again and again, funneling into a nightmare blizzard of stones, the sun a burning stone falling on me. Doc Sol was the only one I'd chance talking to. But Doc had become unhinged by his reading, reading the other Lefties considered blasphemous and a digression from the difficult work of preparing the way for a socialist state. Doc and I sat in a diner drinking coffee. This was a discussion tainted with such possibilities of apostasy that we couldn't talk in Yetta's candy store. I told Doc about the dream that had become a recurring nightmare and my ostensibly wakeful roaming of the streets quarreling with God. Doc rarely used the word God; he spoke of the principle of organization governing the Universe, the physics regulating the movement of stars and the tides of the oceans. Regarding the evolution of the human conscience, this process was slowest of all and perhaps divinity's most primitive and complex work. Doc, by way of illustration, whistled something, some strange other-worldly music, the likes of which I'd never heard. He looked sad. He said, I think, "Ap-pog-gia-tura." Baffled I chewed on each succulent syllable. Doc said something about music, "A melodic note making a dissonance with its accompanying harmony, rhythmically more potent than the principal note." I was lost. Doc said he'd been reading, among other things, Freud and Jung. I'd never heard the names before. Doc had recently attended my bar mitzvah despite his reservations about such "primitive rituals"; but he'd also attended, many years ago, my briss, much to my mother's relief. That ritual, which took place, I'm told, in the kitchen, was catalogued in Mother's mind as one of my father's most serious delinquencies.

In my mother's cautionary ranting, which my uncle Irwin would categorize as "normal yelling," Mama warned me of my father's addled and dangerous judgment. She described the pink, lovely infant I'd been, laid out on the kitchen table, innocently wriggling and cooing, awaiting circumcision. My father had insisted on the mohel who had circumcised him. Letzky the Mohel, Mama said, was ancient, palsied, blind in one eye, and a drunk. And she said, "Letzky came from Odessa," and she wouldn't "trust him with a dead cat." My father denied that Letzky the Mohel was blind in one eye, "It was just a little milky," and it was only because of his age that the mohel became unsteady after a couple of drinks. Papa maintained that Letzky hadn't been given any schnapps until after his work was done. My father could never explain to himself or anyone else why it was imperative that the bud of my sex should be carved by the same artisan that had unsheathed him. My aunts and grandmother, all the women were banished from the kitchen. The men, Mama said, drank many toasts, getting a little shickered; before she left the kitchen she begged Doc Sol to "keep an eye," although what she expected him to do to keep me from harm I don't know. She didn't laugh, but I laugh as evidently I survived without harm. Two years later when my brother was born my father went to Brownsville once more looking for Letzky the Mohel. My mother threatened divorce. The issue was resolved by Letzky's death. The mohel had made it to his ninetieth year. My brother's circumcision took place in a hospital, "scientific" said Mama, performed by a doctor. On the occasion of my circumcision Doc Sol had given Mama a gift; it was the first book that was to be part of my library, *Plutarch's Lives*, and inside was a five-dollar bill.

In the diner Doc ordered coffee and peach pie with vanilla ice cream for us. Now I was in my thirteenth year and knew that Doc expected me to start reading *Plutarch's Lives*, which had been sitting on the shelf since I was eight days old. I was, however, far gone in Jack London's *Klondike Adventure*. The peach pie and ice cream were delicious. I was relieved that Doc didn't ask questions about *Plutarch's Lives*. I finished the pie and ice cream and told Doc, as best as I could, of my recurrent nightmare and my compulsive wandering and wondering through the streets of strange neighborhoods.

Doc, patient, resourceful, did what he could to make the specialized vocabulary accessible to me; but before he ever got to discussing my nightmare his exegesis of psychoanalytic theory left me as fearful of my "unconscious" as the Jewish slaves must have been of Egypt. I hoped that my soul was more than a bucket of repressions and willed ignorance. I nodded as Doc went on speaking but didn't hear much more; some powerful, soul saving angst blanked me out into an exquisite species of sleep where I continued to wander.

It was not a Jewish street. There were daisies growing among the abandoned automobile tires, rusted cans, broken bottles, and smashed bricks in the lot that lay between tenements, the clotheslines up above flapping sheets, dense as the rigging of the ships of my dreams, the danger I felt was more and other than the danger of my dreams; this world I never made was fascinating and it made my bowels rumble; the garbage stink impervious to anything I might hope, I was no longer inclined to make a distinction between dreaming and what I was seeing. The three boys trudging through the weeds, climbing over and through the motorless rusted chassis of a doorless car were hunting cats.

The three were dressed as I was, in olive drab army fatigue jackets and khaki trousers. On every street the kids seemed to be in uniform. In those first post-World War II years the inexpensive and durable clothing sold by army surplus stores outfitted the young boys of the fourteenth ward and adjacent neighborhoods. The faces of the three boys were intent, like soldiers or hunters. There was a great clanging and a shriek of sirens. The fire alarm boxes had been pulled before there was fire, out of some instinct for celebratory bedlam, and to drive the alley cats from their hiding places. I'd been wandering for almost a year, hiding in the confusion of my parent's warfare. I could hear, coming from above, like the squeak and caw of birds, the noise of clothesline pulleys. One story up an old woman still as a statue in her window stared at the street boxed in her own silence. One boy climbing through the frame of the doorless car had a shoeshine box with a cloth strap slung over his shoulder. In one hand he held a garbage can lid that he pounded with a stick. The other two boys had cornered a cat in some thick foliage that flourished on brick dust and gasoline fumes. Two of the boys took aim and threw their rocks at the cat. As they threw their rocks the boy with the shoeshine box slung over his shoulder paused in his pounding of the garbage can lid and grunted. The pigeons between rooftops floated serenely. The old woman in the window looked down, indifferent, beyond judging or judgment. When the stones began to fly in my direction I felt prescient; a piece of brick and a rock fell near my feet. Some apprehensible scrap of dream made me scan the lot for the shadow of the rabbis.

But the stones flying at me were not launched by the rabbis of the dream; what whizzed by my head were, I felt, without having the words to name it, agents of Karma, for something I had done or would inevitably do. This was not my block, not my street. When the boys throwing rocks decided that I would be more interesting prey there was no need for discussion, all seemed to know it at once as a piece of brick veered in the air and came at me. The narcoleptic musings that had taken me to this street didn't alter my alertness. I knew when to fight and when to run. These boys were not, I assumed, among the more promising sociopaths, those who, as a rite of passage, would yell at a police car slowly cruising by, "Taxi, Taxi" and then run like hell to avoid getting smacked around by the cops they'd taunted. The boys intent on killing the cat or cracking my skull were just playing. I joined the game. The rock I threw at the shoeshine box boy he deflected, using the garbage can lid as a shield. The rock rang off the metal. I ducked and dodged rocks. As I ducked I swept up a rock and threw side arm at one of the boys facing me. It caught him in the midsection. His eyes closed, his mouth opened, and he folded into the weeds. I saw the shoeshine boy put down his shine box and garbage can lid, pick up a short flat board, and place on it a tin container of shoeshine polish. He lit the can of polish with a match and a flame shot up like a rocket. Using the short flat board as a catapult he launched the flame at me. Brilliant, burning it arched over my head and landed in a pile of debris stacked against the back of a building. I watched the bags of garbage and rotting fruit crates ignite. The sudden bright sharp pain in my right thigh made me stumble. I glimpsed more than three boys throwing rocks. A troop of kids who'd tarried behind the first three had arrived and they were all throwing rocks at me. An infinitesimal pause, nothingness, dark, light, ringing in my ears and silence. Turning, I found I was still on my feet and all the sounds of the world were muffled. The rocks were raining down all around me. The screaming of the boys, the sirens, the garbage can lids that some of the boys crashed together like cymbals, the flames creeping up the side of the building, all was muffled as though performed as a meditative rite, and in that stillness I saw the story that was happening and knew if I wanted to keep it I'd have to run.

My hearing returned two days later. The top of my head took fourteen stitches. When I angled a hand mirror behind my shaven head and peered into the mirror hanging on the wall above the kitchen sink I could see that my head resembled a globe map, the stitched furrows indicating the intricate pattern of my journey. The police had taken me and one other boy to the emergency room of Greenpoint Hospital. The firemen were able to subdue the fire in a ground floor corridor of the abandoned produce warehouse. A social worker was dispatched to my house to talk to my parents. She was a pretty young woman who looked perpetually startled but undaunted. I limped for several days, the deep purple, grapefruit-sized bruise on my left thigh lingered longer than it took for me to regain my natural gait. I looked sufficiently wounded to give Papa pause and he smashed the kitchen table instead of me. At first I heard Mama's normal yelling as something subdued and thoughtful, in contrast to her anguished face; when my hearing returned, and intermittently through the years she recapitulated the shriek, and in the piercing higher decibels I gained a truer appreciation of her damnation of my adventure.

A year passed. My parents were in rare agreement. My wayward tendencies alarmed them and all the Lefties crowding into our kitchen. All were gathered to help. Mama served coffee. She had made cheese and potato blintzes and rugelach. There was a bowl of fruit set out on the table and Papa's bottle of Slivovitz. I was seated at the head of the table, and told by my father to "listen." My mother repeated "listen" whenever she passed and refilled a coffee cup. Yetta who had left Julie in charge of the candy store bent to me and said "Keep an open mind." Uncle Irwin said, "No one here wishes you harm." Leo Levitch sat at the table and appeared as always at the point of tears. Big Mike turned sideways so he could fit through the kitchen door. I thought that Doc Sol was about to say something to me, but Papa shot him a look, and Doc gave me no more than an empathetic glance.

The unintended consequence of my attendance at the settlement house (to keep me off the street, as the social worker had recommended) were many hours spent in the arts and crafts room where, over the year, I had amassed a portfolio of drawings and tempera paintings. Vincent Benedetto, a serious artist who was the instructor two evenings a week, had arranged a scholarship for me and two other boys at the Art Student's League. We were to attend a life drawing class every Saturday at the League for the next year. Mr. Benedetto, a kind and very demanding teacher had smiled when he told me that the captions I'd scrawled beneath my drawings were more accomplished than the drawings, and he recommended that I read Emile Zola; he said, "You'll have a good time." The hair on my head had grown back and my picture, along with the other two boys who'd won scholarships, was in the Sunday Daily Mirror.

My parent's gratification at finding my picture in the newspaper and all the laudable connotations of the word scholarship quickly turned into something dubious, fraught with the probability of downfall.

Everyone at the table was looking at me. This, I thought, is an important occasion. My parents must have talked, planned. It was pleasant to think of them conferring in bed, and me, important enough to be the occasion of surcease from their war. Yetta was allowed to speak first. She said, "Chekhov was a doctor." I didn't get it. But after, when I began to understand, for at least six years I was compelled in part as an exorcism, to title every story I attempted to write, "Chekhov Was A Doctor." I could tell from the look on Doc's face that even he couldn't dismiss the imperative implicit in Yetta's invocation, "Chekhov was a doctor." I did sense in Yetta's alarm, as in my parent's panic and the Lefties dread over my "artistic tendencies" that the romance I'd entered could take me away from any true concern with the commonweal. I was in danger of becoming something monstrous. I took a bite of a pear. The restraint had broken down. They were all talking to me, at me, at once. Everyone concerned with me. Attentive though I was, I couldn't be certain that I wasn't still in my special sleep, disobedience alive in the pocket of my mind. My mind a thing of interest to everyone. Big Mike putting down shots of Slivovitz with my father said, a mouthful of potato blintzes and apple sauce on his chin, "What! You want to be a debutante? Potchkeh making poetry—eppes, pictures?!" "Look" said Uncle Irwin in his most solicitous voice, "You want to be an idealist at least do something real for people, something practical." "The kid's got a mouth" said Papa; "He got words—a labor lawyer with that mouth he could be—do something to help working people, instead of potchkehring around artistic, which is already half a bum!" Yetta screamed "Please." My father hollered, "OK, everybody shut up, Yetta speaks!" "Listen," she said, "like I said, first Chekhov was a doctor, he healed people, fixed broken bones, then after he wrote stories. He was only a liberal, but his heart was in the right place. Even Chekhov himself said 'Medicine is my legitimate wife, literature my mistress.'" I thought I saw Doc smile, as inadvertently Yetta had given my waywardness encouragement. "Besides," said Uncle Irwin, "in a capitalist society to be an artist you can wind up starving, not able to help yourself let alone anyone else. You'll end up staring into your pipick." "Ah" said Leo suddenly, his face gushing love, and clapping me on the shoulder, "in a society like this you should wear your poverty like a badge of honor." Papa rose out of his chair. The look on his face made everyone quiet. Mama stood still holding the coffee pot and bit her lower lip. Yetta covered her eyes. "Leo," Papa said, trembling, "you tell my son shit like that and I'm gonna throw you out of the window." Leo looked at the kitchen window. We were four stories up from the street. Some kind of reproach alive since he floated in his mother's womb was beating the hell out of him, and once more he'd ventured an answer and it was wrong; also, as Leo knew, Papa never indulged in metaphorical language for its own sake. He could see himself flying through the window, falling the four stories down through the air to the waiting pavement; and as Leo wiped his eyes and blew his nose into his shirttail Papa turned his wrathful face to me. It was my fault, my wayward tendency had put Leo's life in jeopardy and Papa would never be able to forgive me.

Again last night I wrestled Papa. A street brawl not without comic affect, I nearly laughed while trying not to suffocate in his bear hug; my bones about to crack, pedestrians got out of the way. Papa squeezed my backbone until my spine almost touched my belly button, as he also reassured the scurrying pedestrians who gave us wide berth, that they had nothing to fear; and he pleaded his case as a father, inviting the fleeing strangers to make comment, judge the son who denied his father his most fundamental right and pleasure. The argument, if you can call it an argument, struck me as an aria from which I wasn't immune even after I awoke: the aria Doc had once characterized as "Argumentum ad populum."

Four years later, after "hello" Papa picked up the argument again. I'd written my first "Chekhov Was A Doctor" story and harbored two more, one that I didn't know as a story yet.

I was still in uniform. Just back from Korea, it was my first day as a civilian. Papa kissed me on the mouth, wept with joy, lifted me up in the air, and returned me to my feet on the sidewalk. My face went hot. I hated how he made my heart pound. The street was festive; it was spring. Across the way, in front of the pet shop window filled with lemon and lime colored finches fluttering in the air, the chess hustler stood before two chess boards set up on portable stands, his two opponents and the half dozen spectators oblivious to the honking taxis rumbling down the avenue, or the vendor set up a few yards away, with his wind-up menagerie of tiny rearing elephants, wee lions, wall-eyed dinosaurs, and red-jacketed monkeys clapping tambourines. The zoo clickety-clacked over the pavement, around the feet of passersby and several gawking kids.

Papa hauled me across the street by the elbow, halting traffic, giving the finger to the cursing cab driver. He insisted on taking me on the same tour of "where the Hoovervilles used to be" that he marched me through when I was ten. We paused in the argument that had gone on for miles of streets, years. I said I was hungry. He smiled and elbowed us through the crowded street. I'm not sure how the quarrel about the weather started. Who said it first. Some expression of gratitude for the warmth, winter finally gone. He said, "What-do you know from cold?" I said, "It was thirty-below in Korea." He said, "In 1935 the streets were ice, inside like outside, you could see your breath in the kitchen," and shoved through the crowd to the souvlaki stand. The aroma of sausage, lamb, and fried onion was wonderful.

Eating, we were far gone in a small eternity; he asked, "Tender?" "Good," I answered. "Good?" he hollered, "Good? It's delicious!" he shouted. "The food is in my mouth, No?" He's telling me the taste in my mouth! "Listen" I said, forcing him back on his former premise, back, back to what he said before we got to the souvlaki joint, to what he was saying four years ago in the kitchen, before the Far East when I was a civilian and a virgin. "Davey?" he said, inflecting my name into a question as though I still needed his tickle to exist, "you there?" "Yeah," I said then and now. Again and again.

But I wasn't sure, was it the scent, the perfume in the air I could no longer detect, a Far East, my life a thing in itself. I'd lied to the recruiting officer about my age; I wasn't quite eighteen when I enlisted for the three-year stint. I'd also lied to myself. It wasn't only my mother exceeding normal yelling and my younger brother Jacob, lost in a narrative his mind made of its own accord—my mother and brother well on their way to psychiatrically defined madness while Papa pitied the mystery of illness, swung his baling hook, and gulped Slivovitz. I ran away from home because also, I was in love, and spent too much time in the solitary confinement of the toilet. Helene Levy and I had kissed, fondled, and shuddered for a year. She said she loved me but explained the higher duty to her parents who'd sacrificed for her future. Frenzied as we were she stopped my hands at her waist, wept and said she had to save herself for her husband, who must be a doctor, a lawyer, at least a dentist, and it was clear to her that I would never be one of those. I joined the army to get laid, and ultimately, return to the first draft of "Chekhov Was A Doctor."

FAR EAST

On the troop ship in the mid-Pacific, slung in a hammock cramped between the hammocks stacked above and below me, my helmet on my stomach, my duffel bag at my feet, my guts rode the ocean's swells and before I and the regiment got sick I remembered Helene breathing as though she were undergoing an asthma attack when my hand touched her breast. Her tortured breathing, panic, and remorse drove me to the toilet with the remedy her chastity required.

As the heavy weather gathered force the officers ordered a Short Arm Inspection. Navy personnel preparing food in the ship's galley had discovered that a number of the soldiers assigned to kitchen duty and handling food were afflicted with venereal disease. Some thousand or more soldiers strung out in a labyrinthine line weaving through the intricate steel innards of the ship waited infinite hours, laughing, cursing, falling and vomiting as the vessel, which had once appeared colossal, tossed, a petite iron thing juggled by monumental waves, groaned mightily on the inside, while each trooper waited his turn to fish out his penis, milk it down and have it inspected. Beyond the apparent health concerns it seemed to the endless winding ranks of men staggering, tumbling, hanging on to one another, that this process, the wild dance of staying on one's feet in the display of one's genitals, deep in the topsy-turvy vessel, teeming as an ant hill and bouncing on the tormented sea, the short arm inspection must have some deeper purpose or meaning.

Before I was sickened by the men tossing their guts and after my head collided with a steel rafter, leaving a bump on my forehead, which felt like the pedagogy I was accustomed to: the psychopathology of every day life, what I would have preferred to forget as I was at least profoundly embarrassed if not ashamed, the hot zetz illuming my head reminded me of how I partook of Pearly Cheechko's democratic largesse, letting my head land soft, cushioned on her bosom.

Before Helene Levy there had been Pearly Cheechko. But Pearly had been there for everybody, comforting, self-absorbed. Street game, ritual, rite, the game had been in the street for generations, in my time called "Johnny On the Pony" and a generation later, "Buck-Buck." The ship bucked, some of the tottering recruits speculated that those discovered to have a dose would not be given a twenty-four hour pass to leave ship when we docked at Yokohama.

The rules of Johnny-On-the-Pony required two teams of at least three players each, usually five. One team bent at the waist, arms encircling the waist of the boy in front, bending one's back with arms locked around the mate directly in front, the bent backs formed a bridge. The task of the opposing team was to break the bridge. Which team got to charge first was decided by the toss of a coin. One boy at a time ran across the street, never stopping for traffic, and leaping, came down hard with feet, knees, elbows, or head first, trying to buckle and break the bridge of backs. There was another element to the game; one boy was chosen (eenie-meenie-minie-mo, one potato-two potato) as a pillar and cushion to stand against a wall; the next boy, the first link in the bridge with his head pressed against the gut of the pillar, would clamp his arms around the pillar's waist. As the opposing bodies hurled themselves head or feet first, the pillar, like those who made a bridge of their backs, found out how much he could endure, but unlike those bent in the obeisant posture, the pillar's face showed what was being endured. When the bridge of backs fell the victor's reward was to take their turn being the bridge.

The legend on our street was that once upon a time Detective Ape Lesnovich, bag man for the local precinct, who might have provided paleontologists with living proof of the missing link hypothesis, young Ape Lesnovich had played Johnny On the Pony before the convention of the pillar was introduced to the game and broke his arm in two places. Ape careened off the backs into a brick wall and ricocheted off the pavement. No one telling the story would ever call Ape Lesnovich "Ape" to his face, but everyone who told the story told it as though being flogged, laughter beating the speaker so that the tale, protracted by gasps and staggering, became an accident resembling the accident the telling mimed. Young Ape stood howling in the street, his arm broken at the elbow and wrist hung past his knees; the Johnny-On-the-Pony players ran out into the gutter screaming, stopped traffic, commandeered an ice truck and begged the driver to rush to the emergency room of Greenpoint Hospital. Everyone piled into the cab and onto the flat bed of the truck. They'd sped off and had gone the length of the block, and turned the corner when someone realized that in the excitement and hilarity of the myth being told for the first time they had left Ape standing on the sidewalk.

I don't know whether Pearly Cheechko had originally been commandeered to be the pillar in the Johnny-on-the-Pony contest, but afterward she volunteered, stoic rather than demure; the genesis of her availability was the subject of gossip, which also became myth as she never denied that her father and older brother slept with her, and she tended to her silent mother, who suffered from migraines and diabetes. The year that I went into the service the street was full of talk, everyone shocked because Pearly had set up housekeeping in Greenwich Village with Grace Adams, the social worker who had directed me into the settlement house, where I first amassed the portfolio of drawings that were the beginning of the story that would require more than one lifetime.

Pearly was a terrific handball player. She walked the street like a stevedore looking for trouble, despite her accommodating nature. When she stood against the wall, performing her function as "pillar' during Johnny On the Pony, even in chilly weather, as requested, she removed her jacket so that her ample breasts could be seen in all their glory. Pearly's dark boyish face was another anomaly; as she waited for the boys about to charge across the gutter and leap hurtling against her, often with arms outstretched and hands open and fingers spread to grab, her eyes were rolled up white to heaven like Joan of Arc in repose in the flames, her mouth a lopsided tough guy grin.

Quiet, but without reticence, Pearly would answer any question and it never occurred to her to lie. I became expert at swimming through the air; the gutter whooshed below and I landed using my shoulders, arms, and fluttering feet on the backs and rumps beneath me, slowing my skid, my hands never touched Pearly's breasts, but my head came to rest there, soft, drowsing. Pearly and I exchanged a quick glance of recognition and she tilted her cheek to the top of my head.

The sea was calm when we docked at Yokohama. The ship's cargo of boys spilled out into the street delirious, loud, crowding into taxis and bars, the entrepreneurial pimps and the cabbies guiding the boys to where they wanted to go. What clamored in me wasn't all that different, although I wanted it to be different, but not conspicuous. I hung back, managed an anonymity that I hoped made me invisible as I moved through the boisterous, neon-lit streets carrying my virginity like a bride governed by a mystery I obeyed for reasons that eluded me.

As I turned into a less populated street, a narrow thoroughfare of lights, leading me back to water, I became aware that the shadow that followed me wasn't me. I turned on him quick, ready to swing. The young, Japanese gentleman apologized and bowed slightly from the waist. He said, "I beg your pardon, sir," his accent a serviceable alloy of patrician New England and BBC English. He wore a tweed jacket, white shirt, gray tie, charcoal colored trousers and black beret; monochromatic except for the avidity of his bright eyes which distilled the neon lights and his brilliant, knowing smile. I felt ridiculous. He asked if I had a cigarette. I gave him one. We both lit up and smoked. He studied me; something in the attitude of his attentive stare conveyed the sense that he examined me only to confirm what he already knew. He looked at my right leg trouser pocket, beginning to split at the seam, bulging with the *East of Eden*, and said "What, sir, if you don't mind my asking, are you reading?" My hand went to my swollen pocket, the fabric tearing at my thigh, and it occurred to me that if I appeared too ragged and encountered some chicken-shit MP I could be ordered back to the ship. "Steinbeck" I said. "Oh," he said, "I see," and there was something kindly and condescending in the perfect pitch and pronunciation of his voice. I wanted to get away, fearful of what he could see. Some judgment of this stranger could persuade me that my aspirations were hopeless. He launched into a tribute to Thomas Mann as the indispensable light for a young man. He asked me my name. I told him. He said he called himself "Harry," named for the American president who'd reported that the equanimity of his sleep hadn't been disturbed by his decision to drop an atomic bomb on Hiroshima. "Imagine," Harry said, "such strength of character." I said nothing. I'd nodded my head when he spoke of Mann as I recognized the name of an author I hadn't read.

I bought him a pack of cigarettes. We walked a maze of streets; actually I followed, though I walked beside him and listened for the better part of an hour while he lectured, proffering a reading list he insisted was intrinsic to my growth. Harry anticipated every question I didn't ask. He reassured me that eventually I would be equal to the texts that I now feared too difficult, and even at the outset I'd gather enough to make my reading worthwhile. Within forty minutes I became fearful of losing him in the narrow turning streets before I'd heard the names of works essential to what I'd need to know before I could write the story I had to write. I was dependent upon and repelled by his voice, a voice not implicated in what it knew; Harry seemed a ghost, and as much as I might need him I was anxious that Harry, without malice, might be contagious.

What he said to reassure me (again without my needing to ask) and identify himself as a mortal person was as plausible and eccentric as history. The neon-tinted moonlight bent his back into the posture of prayer as he told me that he was born in San Francisco and spent his adolescence during World War II in an internment camp in California, where his mother died. In the last year of the war, he, along with his widowed father, an avid gardener and lover of European literature, had been repatriated to Japan.

He suggested a bar. We drank saki. I found it was as efficacious as Slivovitz and was happy to pay for our drinks. I bought him a carton of Lucky Strikes, which the bartender discretely slipped into a brown paper bag. Harry urged that I not display the thick wad of bills that I'd taken from my pocket. I realized then the novelty of being a rich American. I had a month's pay in my pocket. Half of it was in military pay currency and half in dollars. One dollar in MPC was worth five hundred yen at the exchange and eight hundred yen on the black market; a civilian American dollar was worth much more. Harry was telling me how Thomas Mann had described the affinity the artist shared with the criminal, the necessary outsider status and alienation made vision possible. The wealth in my pocket, the saki induced tropical weather in my head, these unaccountable gifts promised rare insights that would become clear if I kept myself open to the night's adventure. I didn't interrupt Harry as I remembered my father eating as though every pleasure were an act of theft and I couldn't glean the connection between Harry's talk and the memory of my father at the table. Years later, when it struck me that all the authors Harry insisted were crucial to my education (Mann, Lawrence, Dostoevsky, Céline, Pound and Eliot) were anti-Semites, I concluded that this learning was not vengeance on his part, the irony of the circumstance was not worth his mentioning since giving up western literature was not an option for me; and he'd been talking and chain smoking for a long while about the advantage and necessity of being an outsider/criminal in order to see what an artist might see. As a judge would clarify the charge to an indicted burglar, "Breaking and Entering," I'd take what I need but never shake the memory of Shakespeare's witches in Macbeth cooking up their brew and declaring the indispensible ingredient, "the liver of blaspheming Jew."

I came to in the back of the rolling cab without any idea of how long I'd been out. I didn't feel sick or hurt and it would be two decades before I'd have any awareness of the distinction between passing out and blacking out. My absence I accepted as respite, an aspect of the adventure facilitated by saki. My eyes were open; they may have been open all during the lost time. Harry was apologizing for the length of the journey, assuring me that I'd see that the trip and the preparations were necessary. I couldn't tell whether Harry's courtesy precluded his acknowledging my absence (while my arms and legs had worked, and I spoke, saying what?) or he concurred with my sense of a trance in which I'd decided that I couldn't repudiate this part of my life, even in years to come when my spirit would have to pay something usurious, and I couldn't avoid terrible judgment and punishment; but looking at myself rocking gently in the back seat of the cab, seated next to Harry,

I saw I was already dressed for that occasion, formally, in a blue, pin-striped suit, white shirt, narrow blue tie, and a camera hung from a leather strap slung around my neck.

Discreetly as possible my fingers found my pockets and I discovered that the wad of bills had thickened and grown into both trouser pockets and in a brand new leather billfold inside the silk-lined pocket of my suit jacket.

Harry slipped a tiny key into my hand, patted a small, expensive looking suitcase propped between our knees, and said, "Your uniform and a bottle of scotch are in there. The house we are going to will welcome suitable western clientele, but never soldiers, sailors, or marines under the rank of major, and even the brass must be attired in civilian clothing. I will explain that you are a visiting journalist, young and accomplished, and please, I must have confidence that you will maintain this fiction or you'll create serious trouble for me."

As we got out of the cab Harry asked for money and I gave him a half-inch thick wad of yen. He nodded.

The moon and stars retired behind the greater dark; the quiet, and the street with the several modest dwellings, the windows infused what could be the very first or the last light of day, the night and everything in it a medium of discretion that Harry knew how to negotiate, my head lit up with a momentary paranoia, the lurid vision of Harry leading me to the alley where I would have my head broken and my pockets emptied dissipated within the moment; the noria in the running stream at the side of the house turned, the small buckets on the rotating wheel plopping water back into the stream a calming mantra, and I considered that Harry had infallibly touched the place of my inchoate faith as he participated in furthering the possibilities of my language, the more troubling worry, the embarrassment; did Harry know as he knew and assessed my reading, that I was a virgin.

We entered the interior of a house made of blond wood and white paper walls that slid softly revealing cubicles of twilight. Before Harry conferred with an older woman who looked like Queen Victoria swaddled in a giant orange pillow, he whispered to me that "the girls in this house don't have many miles on them." Harry's automotive analogy hurt my heart and I don't know whether my sudden hatred of his knowingness did it, but within the moment I saw him, mandarin, neurasthenic, wasting from some exquisite disease which was not a subject of particular interest to him, and plush pillowed Queen Victoria bright as a beetle glide by a shifting white wall that rippled like silk and they were gone.

The room had the fragrance of sandalwood. The girl walking toward me wore a rose-colored robe and her black hair fell past her shoulders, her every movement serene music that made me dumb and required protocols I couldn't imagine. She bowed. I bowed. She said, "Reiko," which I assumed was her name. I said my name was Davey. She gestured for me to put down the suitcase. Her hands pantomimed instruction and I undressed. I put on the white bathrobe she handed me. Our heads bumped as I tried to prevent her from kneeling; she laughed, kneeled, and put slippers on my feet. She took me by the hand and led me through the silken walls of faint light that slid away at her touch and led me down a flight of steps into a lagoon of mist. She took off her robe and slippers. I did the same.

In the quiet water her beauty was bearable. We washed one another. My hands parted streams of mist and looking down into the water I could see my toes blooming into floral shapes. I could hardly hold the thought that all this was available for money; and what unspeakable necessity brought Reiko here?—and me here?—a universal John, stunned and grateful for the remedial grace of her trade; and yet we might have been children floating and touching in the asylum of a womb where we invented another ephemeral language to serve the moment of my dream, and I began to hope, hers.

Back in the perfumed cradle, Reiko's look of surprise may have been a requirement of her art, but in the throes I experienced life imitating art as a sacramental principle. I was no longer a virgin and oddly naked beyond the reach of irony. Like a mollusk shorn of its shell I lay there, damp and gleaming.

For a long while we held each other and drowsed. The primacy of speech went wherever it went for renewal. After a time I wanted her again, and again, and again.

And then I needed to tell her. The words I spoke were the first words ever spoken. Her smiling face conveyed her faith that the sounds I made had meaning.

Each time, after lovemaking, in the respite akin to waking, I tried to say it again in many ways. The breath of the first syllables prehistoric music introducing me to the world.

I stood still, obedient as a child being diapered as Reiko

folded and arranged between my legs and around my waist the soft, white cloth. She removed my bathrobe and smiled. She held up both hands and wiggled her ten fingers. Holding up both hands she laughed and folded the pinkie and thumb of her left hand so that she was displaying eight fingers, nodding her head until I understood. Standing legs akimbo in my diaper loincloth, I surmised morning (it may have been noon) and counted one through eight. She laughed and led me by the hand through the white silken walls the lovely young women parted, laughing and applauding, and at last I understood that we had made love eight times. Diapered for modesty's sake, I strutted, nearly naked, and knew I looked splendid without my clothes.

Reiko's smile, like the laughter and applause of the other half-dozen brilliantly robed young women reminded me of my mother's "kvelling" when early in my elementary school career I had brought home a report card with all A's. Applause surrounded me. I bowed and held up my hands for silence.

I tried to say it again to Reiko through the small crowd of women where I hoped I'd find a trustworthy interpreter. What I was saying, had been saying, tried to say after lovemaking, was that although this was something available to me for money it was nevertheless a miracle; the miracle was in no way diminished; indeed, I was willing to pay in a lifetime of devotion, work, art, heroics, marriage—who could say what recompense was worthy, appropriate. They applauded again, and laughed. One of the young women stepped forward, meeting my gaze directly; she seemed to understand, not so much from my words, but through her keen sense of my agonist delirium, the sheen of my dazed face; she had seen it before. She said something to the others and they surrounded and guided me back to the frameless deep bed that lay close to the floor; the interpreter whispered an indecipherable sum in my ear. I found my trousers folded neatly over the back of a wooden chair. From one of the pockets I retrieved an inch-thick wad of yen and placed it into the palm of the beauty who appeared to understand and had been selected as an adept of the requisite comity.

They glided away. Next to the bed, on top of a small cabinet, was a bowl of fruit and a bottle of wine.

Reiko and I bathed again. And made love again. Intermittently I attempted to utter it all. Her face insinuated calm. Hours passed. She spoon-fed me a bowl of soup. We slept. We made love. After lovemaking I held the palm of her hand to my lips and inhaled the scent.

When she led me again, on parade in my diaper, the silken walls of light parted at the hands of the young women as before, and this time the applause was softer, as in the giving of an honorarium.

We were seated in a circle on the floor at a low table. The beauty who had functioned as interpreter indicated by the sweep of her hand that I had a choice of champagne, beer, saki, or scotch. I drank the scotch. Standing at the center of the room was Queen Victoria in her great luminous robe of beetle's hue, plump with dominion, neither smiling nor frowning, presiding without saying a word. The young women assembled around the table were attentive, as though about to receive instruction. The interpreter poured me another scotch and said, "Reiko love you long time, three days now. You happy?" I roared "Yes!" "You want?" she asked gesturing toward Reiko. Embarrassed by my shouting, surmising that my loudness was inappropriate to the dignity of the occasion, I nodded my head "yes" vigorously.

The man who appeared from behind a screen adjacent to the circle of tables moved with the alacrity of a butler steeped in knowledge he no longer needed to remember, it was his confident functioning that made the world cohere, maintained civility, and that modicum of reason of which the species is capable. Queen Victoria's regent held out a royal blue belted bathrobe for me to wear. I got to my feet. He helped me into the robe and said softly, "Please you'll want to wear this." His voice assumed the tone of venerable and intimate service, his hands tying the belt around my waist and touching my shoulder reassuringly, not unlike a tailor of the utmost integrity, concerned with above all else, getting the perfect fit for me. He was a middle-aged Westerner, white-haired, tall, smiling and happy in the authority he assumed. He wore a pinstriped suit very much like the one Harry had acquired for me. Despite the vaguely British air of his speech I sensed something American in his presumption. He spoke to me in confidence, so no one else could hear. "You are very young, although youth is not a crime." "So are they," I said as softly as I could, nodding toward Reiko and the women gathered around the table in meditative postures. "Well" said the regent glancing at Reiko appreciatively, "If you really want to learn what it means to be human you'll have to learn Reiko's language." And he went on to describe a paradise of connubial care, praising Reiko's thrift, culinary art, patience and beauty. The regent mentioned a sum that would allow me to "lease" Reiko for three months, and if then I wished a long-term arrangement we could renegotiate terms and at that point, if I desired, the house would take on the expense of a surgeon to render Reiko round-eyed.

My screaming startled me, and brought the presence of a modest mountain moving with the inexorable grace of Birnam Wood closing in on Macbeth; the mountain was dressed in a tuxedo and the impartiality of his face, looking down, didn't encourage inquiry, even if he understood English. The regent and the sumo mountain flanked me on both sides. I was still screaming, "Don't touch her eyes." I glanced at Reiko. She lowered her head, as though I was a child throwing a tantrum and my behavior was her disgrace. The regent went on intoning the financial terms for removing Reiko from the house. I requested permission to return to the twilight crib to check my pockets for cash, the suitcase for the bottle of scotch, and the camera. I figured I could make a good faith down payment with the scotch, camera, and the cash I had left. I could arrange to have my allotment checks sent to Reiko so that in a year's time she would be free to go, and if she wished, I could rejoin her when I was once again a civilian.

The regent nodded. The sumo mountain released my shoulder. I made my way back over the matted byway where I had recently paraded and found that the camera was gone from the suitcase, but the bottle of scotch was there, and from the pocket of the pants neatly folded over the wooden chair I dug out the last quarter-inch thick roll of Yen.

Walking back I noted that the suitcase had been opened, maybe someone saw my uniform. The deception, my being a soldier, perhaps they knew and my status as a GI, Private first class dogface queered everything.

I asked the regent if Harry could join our discussion. He might be able to facilitate a deal. The regent said, "Harry?" I said, "Yes, the gentleman I arrived with." The regent said, "That person left four days ago, shortly after you got here." With the bottle of scotch in one hand and a fistful of yen in the other I began to dance around. I needed to explain and I didn't want the mountain's hands on me. I ran, dodged, nimble as a kid playing tag and shouted the terms I could manage, displaying the bottle of scotch, the money in my fist; I swore a sacred vow—I'd make installment payments over the next year—or two if necessary. The regent said, "This is not within your means." I continued my dance, shouting the terms I could muster. The mountain stalked me. Reiko, the other women, and Queen Victoria disappeared from the room in a flourish of swirling robes. The regent constraining his exasperation at my lack of understanding, his revulsion for the buffo opera that was me repeated, "Young man, this is simply beyond your means—you should go quietly." I guessed that the regent saw my lack of money as a deficiency of character; as I ducked the mountain's grasping hand I thought the regent might be on to something. I remained as I was, a boy, arithmetic a sea as antithetical to me as Poscidon's ocean to Odysseus. But hadn't Reiko and I, despite this reckoning, been one flesh in timelessness; shouldn't that matter, hadn't we entered into something beyond calculation? And then I began to calculate. If only Reiko could testify to this—if only I could make love to her one more time I might be able to reconcile myself to losing her, reconcile myself to loss, the tragic, and live a truly thoughtful life. I chased after her and the mountain snatched at me. I tried to say something to the effect that I wasn't dismissing the importance of quantitative reckoning, only that the mortal two years that I would commit to making payments should count for some consideration. The mountain grabbed my wrist. My fist opened like a flower and the money floated down. I was off my feet and in the air as he held and swung me in a circle around his head. The flight washed whatever argument I had been about to offer and with the hand still grasping the bottle of scotch I swung hard as I could at the fixed point of the shining bald head. The mountain and I fell.

In the heat, outside the Mess Hall, the flies buzzing around my head, I'd almost become acclimated to my own stink as I separated edible from inedible garbage. Master Sergeant Crawford checked periodically to make sure that I plunged my arm deep enough into the garbage can to retrieve from the rancid creamed chipped beef, rinds, bones, and rotting fruit, any cigarette butts and cardboard containers that the troopers had scraped from their food trays as they filed out of the

Mess Hall. I was responsible for removing anything that could interfere with the digestion of pigs, as the military sold and or contributed the swill to farmers, and the pigs, it was said, thrived on army slop.

I washed and scoured the garbage cans until they gleamed. Before separating edible from inedible garbage, I washed pots and pans in the Mess Hall. I cleaned out the Mess Hall grease trap. I dug latrine pits where Sergeant Crawford entombed his cigarette butts. A late sunny afternoon found me on the simmering metal roof of the Mess Hall rubbing away rust spots with sandpaper.

Sometime during the third or fourth week, lightheaded, cooking on the roof, I maneuvered to a rust spot in a patch of shade, smelled myself and associated my stench with my having rationalized having something that money should never be able to buy. Caught in endlessness this was as far as my guilt took me; I couldn't say that if money were the only means of my access to Reiko I wouldn't do it again. I was grateful for the clouds passing over the sun and the breeze. Dizzy and stinking on the roof, I turned my head up, watched the rushing clouds, and riding the roof I had the sensation of flying through the sky. I studied the changing shape of a cloud, closed my eyes to the glare. The sunlight penetrated my eyelids and I saw Reiko's face. I recalled that the only way to get beyond the enthrallment of her beauty was to make love; and then in the peaceful eddies it had been possible to think and speak; but we didn't share a language, and I don't know why, but suddenly I thought that perhaps the survival of Reiko's inner life required that she should never be susceptible to abandon, however aptly her art mimed love.

On the roof, a haze before my eyes, fat drops of sweat hung from my earlobes and the tip of my nose. My left shoulder ached. The mountain had used my left arm as a tether as he swung me about. My ribs and chest hurt when I sneezed and breathed deeply. I never saw the mountain rise, or his back up, if he had any, but I was whacked across the back of the neck, thumped against the floor and my lights went out.

The two MP's found me in an alley near a sailor who had been dumped on his face. The MP's nudged me with their feet, yanked me upright, dragging me until I came to and tried to walk under my own power. I noticed that I was in uniform. Disheveled, shoelaces untied, my pants torn at the knees and side pockets, but in uniform.

Captain Roscoe, company commander at the base in Tokyo where I took company punishment and waited for a decision regarding my possible court martial, looked me up and down and drawled, "I didn't know they could stack shit that high. Still, you're one lucky bastard. If you had been found out of uniform the charge would not be AWOL but desertion and then your sorry ass would be lookin' at thirty years. Did your poor mama have any children that lived?"

Each day, before first light, I stood at attention in my fatigues, at the center of the quad; alone except for Sergeant Crawford, in moonlight; and he would bawl, an inch from my face, dampening my cheeks, "'Cruit," short for "recruit," "Your soul may belong to Jesus but your ass belongs to me. On this fine day you will commence with the grease pit, then pots and pans, you will separate edible from inedible garbage, and it will behoove you to dig a five foot long, five feet wide, five feet deep trench so that you may bury the debris you will police from the company grounds. At the close of day, you may peel the peels, making sure those on KP have not wasted precious food on the skin of potatoes, and in sweet twilight you will hasten to the Mess Hall roof and sand away any rust or blemish."

On the Mess Hall roof, I ogled the rushing hot lava of heaven streaming above my head and contemplated the vicissitudes of my afterlife. From the spit-drenched diatribes Sergeant Crawford screamed in my face before first light I concluded I still had a soul, which concerned him, and he, according to his lights was working for my betterment.

One hot endless day Sergeant Crawford standing below on the earth bellowed up in his deep raspy baritone that I wouldn't be court marshaled but shipped to Korea where, the brass believed the armistice would never hold, and my otherwise useless ass would be put in harm's way in the service of my country. In the meantime, before the inevitable hostilities, I was busted, losing my one stripe. I'd take the corresponding pay cut, and before shipping me to Korea, where I'd been headed in the first place, before I violated my twenty-four hour pass, the Army would be certain to change my MOS, that is my military occupational specialty. My MOS was no longer clerk typist, privileged duty, but now I was a body and fender man and I'd work in a motor pool.

Dizzy, lightheaded, flying on the roof, I'd grasped the idea of my reprieve, touched by Sergeant Crawford's concern for me. I toppled face first from my perch in the small pool of shade, and broke my fall by thrusting out my arms and pressing my hands on the burning roof. I howled. Bounced like hot grease on a skillet back to the puddle of shade. I looked at my blistered palms, a cluster of grapes bubbling up in the palm of each hand, I waved both hands in the breeze above my head. I could see Sergeant Crawford, knees buckling, laughing like hell, as he watched my anagogic twitching in the wine colored shade that descended from my hands waving in the sky, in what must have appeared as obeisance.

In the new foreign country no one shot at me. Each night I traveled in the dream I would dream forever, the scent of Reiko recognizable in the longings she became; though I was nagged by the sense of having forgotten something essential. In the morning before the recorded bugle blew reveille, Queen Victoria in her Kabuki mask shook me from sleep. After not very long my sleep dispensed with her employment and I forgot her. I also forgot remembering that the war didn't happen. From time to time we were required to play war games. Not all the hardship was simulated. We marched, climbed up and down mountains under full packs, M1 rifles slung over our shoulders; we camped in tents on hard ground in the cold, the foulest weather chosen for these exercises; but the maneuvers felt like the price of entitlement. For the most part it was an odd, cushy life. Every GI suddenly, for the first and perhaps the only time in his life, a prince. The eagle shat at the end of each month and every soldier's pocket was stuffed with a fortune, the omnipotent American dollar, the richest coin in the world. Fate's survivors, living lavishly between the ordained slaughters, urban peasant or redneck, we were chosen for a privileged existence. Even those who had grown up hungry, shoeless, cold, now had servants and complained of the difficulty of getting reliable help.

Koreans, grown men and boys cleaned and prepared the barracks for inspection. They did the laundry, spit shined our boots, made up our bunks in the morning, and pulled KP duty. All this cost each GI a dollar or two a month. The Koreans who had such employment considered themselves among the fortunate; what they earned was sufficient to support a large family and a host of relatives.

The casualties among the troops were primarily venereal. I remained faithful to something I couldn't name. There was a small but well stocked library on the base. I taped to the inside of my wall locker door lists of new words and their definitions. Walking from the barracks or the Mess Hall to the motor pool, my life between reveille and taps settled into a routine. I'd look out into the bay. I had never seen anything like it before. When the tide was out the ocean disappeared. To the very brink of the horizon, where the sky rested on the periphery of the earth, some three miles out, mud flats, alluvial manna puckered and breathing in the mire all the way to the boundary of infinity. When the Red Sea parted did the path resemble this? The laboring shadows in the distance were Mama-sans scavenging for shellfish and other edibles in the exposed ocean floor; the work had to be done swiftly, before the tide came in.

The Motor Pool, a Quonset hut, made of metal, was about half the size of a football field. Inside, the two and a half ton trucks, the three quarter ton trucks, and the jeeps were serviced. Like the maintenance of weapons, this work was not dispensed to the Koreans, although there were three Korean men employed among the twenty GI mechanics, primarily to fetch and carry. The sounds of pounding and human voices echoed as in a cave, reverberating, loud, syllables swelling and exploding like gunshot, everyone had to shout and augment speech with hand signs. Portable radios blared rock and roll adding to the din. No one appeared to require quiet, the tremendous racket seemed a kind sustenance to the men, the noise itself an affirmation. The men gathered around each truck as around some great primal mastodon which they cared for lovingly.

After the first day I went to the PX and bought a box of absorbent cotton and made earplugs. Each morning as I entered the Motor Pool I pressed cotton pellets into my ears. I could discern the intention of the orders shouted at me. Along with the great roaring hum and clanging like thunder, I felt my heart beating in my ears, as though I were becoming amphibian and learning to feel under a depth of water.

Master Sergeant Russell's sinuous purr made its way through the percussive reverberations. On the very first day he made himself clear to me. The first moment was surprising because of his rugged good looks. The men worshiped him. He was a combat veteran who had been awarded many medals, which he would only wear under orders during various obligatory military ceremonies. The creases in his khaki trousers were razor sharp, his brass belt buckle shined like a mirror, the whole lean muscular form of the man remained starched and immaculate throughout the day in defiance of all weather. His face was a dream of American innocence, rugged, righteous, and clear-eyed, untainted by the carnage he had known. Or at least these were my projections as I stood in awe, before Master Sergeant Russell.

I had confessed to Sergeant Russell right off that in spite of my MOS I was not a body and fender man, didn't know anything about it, indeed didn't have a driver's license, living in New York as a civilian I had availed myself of public transportation and hadn't found it necessary to learn how to drive. Sergeant Russell looked perplexed, then irritated, as if my calm were a form of impudence. I hesitated, wasn't sure how or if I should try to explain that I hadn't meant to appear insubordinate; but something blocked me from justifying myself and then I thought that after all there was something in me that was insubordinate. Sergeant Russell said in partial answer to the conundrum I represented, "A fuck-up. They sent me a fuck-up." "They" I assumed meant the Brass, and the Brass functioned with the whimsy of Greek deities, while the heroic among humans struggled to make some sense of it. I thought I heard a corporal who was standing close by with a lit match in his hand, waiting to light the cigarette that dangled from Sergeant Russell's lip, mutter, "Jew York." This designation offered by the corporal to the sergeant as an explanation to demystify the ineffable, but I wasn't sure whether that was what I heard or what I'd heard was my whispering paranoia, although I came by my paranoia honestly.

When I agreed, without a sign of protest, to work along with the Koreans, fetching and hauling, Sergeant Russell looked troubled. He stared at me waiting for some response I failed to provide, and finally concluding that my acceptance was in some way subversive, he barked that he would keep a close watch on me, and I'd better keep to my duties. I said, "Yes, sir." Sergeant Russell hissed, "Don't call me sir, I work for a fuckin' livin'."

I had my evenings. I had the night and I was content; I was more than content, I was enchanted. I'd come across the work of William Faulkner at the post library and I spent the next year itinerant, wandering along through Joe Christmas's tragic misadventure in *Light In August*, *The Old Man* lost in the flood, followed Addy Budrin's coffin, also swept away in rampaging water in *As I lay Dying*, as I traveled the stately, convoluted, brilliant rhetoric that sounded like God trying to discover his own secrets.

More than a month passed and I considered how the brutalization of the foundling Joe Christmas was the antithesis of the Nativity. Meanwhile along with Mr. Sung, Mr. Kim, and Mr. Shin I hurried to fetch screw drivers, pliers, lug wrench, spanner wrench, learned to identify and carry the filler wrench for changing oil, the breaker bar to break rust and loosen nuts, alligator clips for the charger, pulled the floor jack and carried batteries across the booming length of the Motor Pool and learned that despite the look of perpetual mockery on PFC Glidden's red face, he hadn't actually called me a "creep." I was slow to take offence, slow to understand. I hadn't any awareness of the resentment building in my own dark and I was as surprised as PFC Glidding when I grabbed him by the lapels of his fatigue jacket and slammed him against the side of the Jeep. Several men jumped in and separated us.

Standing before Sergeant Russell I expected that he was about to read me the riot act and that this time I was in deep shit. His face revealed nothing beyond the shadow of a long endured sadness as he pointed at the floor and commanded, "Look at that!" "What?" "That pissant! Open your damn eyes!" I looked at a low platform with four wheels, very close to the floor that I recognized as a device for a mechanic to lie on as he slid himself below the belly of a vehicle. "That," barked Sergeant Russell, "is called a creeper"; and I thought I saw Sergeant Russell almost smile. Slowly it dawned on me: during the elusive forever of the past month while I journeyed Faulkner's language Sergeant Russell had been waiting, not urgently, but baffled, waiting for some sign from me. My ready acceptance of my assignment to work with the Koreans had struck Sergeant Russell as a symptom of some malfeasance or idiocy. The complete absence on my part of any detectable amour propre had alarmed the sergeant and confirmed the forebodings that gave the sad cast to his stern look.

Master Sergeant Russell mitigated my duties by also making me his orderly. This meant that in addition to fetching and hauling tools and parts I would deliver paperwork to the clerk typist at headquarters, purchase cigarettes for him at the PX and bring coffee from the Mess Hall several times a day. I was not allowed to sit down, ever. Neither Sergeant Russell nor Corporal Bickford, who had offered to unravel the mystery of me by whispering in Sergeant Russell's ear "Jew York," ever engaged me in conversation. I had the feeling that their charity was based on the premise that my proximity to them, and especially to Sergeant Russell, was salutary in itself; they conversed and I could overhear whatever it was I was attentive enough to retain and thus, possibly improve myself.

I had reached a point where the weight of whatever I carried provided gratification; the sweat that ran down my back confirmed a sense of growing strength; and if I was demonstrably crazy, I wasn't so much out of my mind as deeper in it, in some strange place.

One day after pulling and lifting a hand truck loaded with a tank of gas and an acetylene torch across the floor, littered with tools and tires, I returned to a grave looking Sergeant Russell, sitting like a heartbroken monarch behind his desk. Corporal Bickford was bent to Sergeant Russell's ear and he appeared to be consoling him. I stood there for some time while I took on sufficient presence to become visible. The rain banging on the vast metal roof was torrential and deafening; wiping sweat out of my eyes I imagined heaven in a promethean frenzy vomiting every tool there ever was or would be, all of it thundering on the roof hastening the end of the known world. The work continued, men bellowed, and exchanged hand signs. The portable radios blared country and western music and rock and roll. As I became visible, and startled Sergeant Russell and Corporal Bickford, I remembered that as I had made my way across the cluttered floor, weaving the loaded hand truck around obstacles, and when necessary lifting it, I'd had a moment of panic. The tremendous noise bombed the place in my mind where I might abide and I stopped, lost, disoriented. It was then that I saw Mr. Kim. He was standing next to a mechanic near the open hood of a truck, pointing at some part of the engine. I stared at Mr. Kim; his eyes met mine for an instant and I had the certain feeling that Mr. Kim emanated his own quiet; I completed my task.

I was irresistibly drawn to studying Mr. Kim. He was aware that I was watching, and if he was affronted by my staring nothing in his face or body language revealed displeasure, or a judgment of any kind. I admired Mr. Kim's face, which expressed only concentration on the task at hand; neither did his face reflect effort nor ease, frustration, nor satisfaction. I considered my own face, which was transparent and could be read by nearly anyone, except on those occasions when my confusion provided a mask of sorts. Almost as an afterthought I saw that Mr. Kim was about five foot three, the fingers of his left hand, except for his thumb were gone, and despite his ability to haul all sorts of very heavy stuff without a sign of strain, his small compact body, the rolled-up sleeves of his fatigue blouse, displayed not the slightest sign of muscle, or the physique of a man who had, in fact, lived a life of hard work.

Eventually I heard from one of the GI mechanics and from the ingratiating Mr. Sung who lived in the same village as Mr.

Kim, that during World War II, at the time of the Japanese occupation, Mr. Kim had assumed the blame for an act he didn't commit to spare a terrified relative, and a Japanese officer, in reprisal, raised his sword and lopped off the four fingers of Mr. Kim's left hand.

Corporal Bickford, having become aware of my presence, pressed his fingers to his shirt pockets. I didn't get it. The corporal patted the pockets of his shirt again and pointed to his lips. I still didn't understand what he was trying to convey. The corporal's face swelled as he yelled at me. Sergeant Russell sat in his chair looking fatalistic. Finally, I understood and bummed a couple of cigarettes for Corporal Bickford and Sergeant Russell and extended my hand for money so that I could go to the PX and buy them a couple of packs of cigarettes.

When I returned with the packs of cigarettes, which I managed to keep dry by keeping my hands clamped around them deep in my trouser pockets, I stood looking like someone who had barely survived drowning, and Sergeant Russell sent me out again into the downpour to deliver a report to the clerk-typist. When I was sent off again after the trip to the clerk-typist to fetch coffee the rain began to subside.

I learned that Mr. Kim, like me, didn't know how to drive; nevertheless with the remaining thumb of his left hand he pointed to the place of failure in a vehicle and the mechanics had come to rely on him as a source of divination. Mr. Kim's thumb with its horny blackened nail and the stumps of fingers drifted infallibly to the place where and why an engine had failed. His English was very limited and he couldn't explain.

There was just the butchered hand and stub of thumb, an unfailing divining rod that even the best mechanics had come to believe in, as they believed in heaven and hell. When the problem was complex, involving two or more places in a vehicle, Mr. Kim's arms rose and fell like a man playing the piano with his fists. Sergeant Russell believed that Mr. Kim's ability to detect what was wrong with an engine was the benign aspect of something diabolical.

Tools were missing. "Stolen," Corporal Bickford said. Sergeant Russell and Corporal Bickford were certain that one or more of the Koreans were responsible for the theft. The other men commented on the legendary stealth and agility of the Korean thieves known as Slicky Boys. One of the men told again the story of the lieutenant in Seoul who had been driving his jeep and had not come to a complete stop until he reached his destination; then he found that the spare tire that had been screwed on to the back of the jeep was gone.

Because of Mr. Kim's wizardry Sergeant Russell and Corporal Bickford questioned him first. They made plain that they believed that he knew which of his countrymen were guilty of the theft. Mr. Kim stood and listened. Corporal Bickford said it was possible that Mr. Kim was the leader of the thieves; the Slicky Boys were probably relatives. Mr. Kim stood, listening, studying their faces and at last said, "Not so." As the interrogation went on and Sergeant Russell waited for a reply from Mr. Kim, Mr. Kim said, "Hungry people sometime number ten." In the pidgin that the GIs and Koreans employed to understand one another, in all things what was "number ten" was the worst and what was "number one" the very best. As I watched the faces of Corporal Bickford, Mr. Kim, and Sergeant Russell I saw a look of distaste curl the sergeant's lips as he stared at Mr. Kim; Sergeant Russell, as he later tried to explain to the corporal, had concluded that Mr. Kim was one who neither required forgiveness nor did he need to forgive, he simply understood. And this too, testified to Sergeant Russell's sense of the fallen world.

I lost sight of Mr. Kim. He must have been working in the far north end of the garage. The concern with the theft of the tools, like the tools themselves, disappeared into a resentful acceptance, a kind of forgetfulness predicated on the expectation that someday the tools would appear again, perhaps in the black market.

I was still searching for a glimpse of Mr. Kim during the morning that I rolled the worn Jeep tires to the storage shed and made a couple of coffee runs to the Mess Hall. Corporal Bickford was tending to Sergeant Russell's hangover. Sergeant Russell, as usual, appeared to be his immaculate, soldierly self, only the dark pockets under his eyes suggested that he was in rough shape. Corporal Bickford ministered to Sergeant Russell seated at his desk, the sergeant's head propped in his right hand, his elbow on the desk, a tableau I passed again and again as I delivered coffee, paperwork, cigarettes; Corporal Bickford was reminding Sergeant Russell to write to his wife. After a time Sergeant Russell said something about his distrust of the desire he felt for the Korean woman he was shacked up with in the village. Corporal Bickford counseled that we must take our pleasures where we find them, and said something suggesting the wisdom of Sergeant Russell's economy, fiscal and emotional.

As the long day continued I heard fragments of a discussion between Sergeant Russell and Corporal Bickford concerning original sin. The two soldiers appeared to be offering one another pardons. Corporal Bickford reminded Sergeant Russell that man's tendency to depravity was the result of Adam's rebellion, and there wasn't a damned thing either of them could do to change that. "Hell's bells" said the sergeant, and he reminded the corporal that the mess had started when the original bitch, Eve, who couldn't stand prosperity, nagged Adam, "Take a bite of the apple honey, take a bite."

Close to chow time Sergeant Russell spoke of the great love of his life, of how he'd been betrayed, and how nothing in his life could have prepared him for this.

As I came and went I heard Sergeant Russell speak of his twenty years of devotion. He testified to the corporal that he had given the best of himself to the relationship, and now he had nothing more to give. Once, toward twilight, Corporal Bickford summoned me out of the void to get a book of matches so he could light the Sergeant's cigarette. I materialized where I had been, standing at ease by the side of the desk. Corporal Bickford said he couldn't argue with Sergeant Russell's conclusion. Sergeant Russell said again, "Hell's bells, twenty years!" I wondered whether Sergeant Russell's wife back in the states had been unfaithful to him; perhaps she'd sent him a "Dear John" letter, or maybe the allure of the Korean woman he was shacked up with was so powerful that in spite of the sergeant's misgivings now he had to acknowledge his estrangement from his wife and reinvent his life whatever the cost in grief and confusion. I felt sympathy for Mrs. Russell, being an Army wife is difficult, given the frequent and long separations. The sergeant had never mentioned children.

As I put the pieces together, coming and going, I gathered that Sergeant Russell, a child of the Depression, from Arkansas, had for the first time in his life been well shod when he went to court his first love, the wife I assumed he now contemplated divorcing. As Sergeant Russell spoke he revealed a special fondness for the words "nomenclature"—as in "the nomenclature of the M1 rifle" and "behooves" as in "it would behoove you mens to study how things work in this man's army."

I had moved on to the *The Sound and the Fury* and as I tried to make sense of the world sounding in Benjy the Idiot's head—landscape, green, fence, hole in the ground, flag and Benjy's moaning—I saw the golf course and my attention wandered. I lifted my head from the book. It was early evening. There was only one other GI in the library and he was asleep in a large leather chair, snoring softly. The library would close in about an hour. It was still close enough to the most recent payday so that the barracks might be deserted and quiet and I could read there. My empathy for Benjy disturbed me. I felt drowsy and haunted by a childlike intuition that I was the avatar of some idiocy that I would never understand. I remembered that when Corporal Bickford looked at me, actually saw me, it was always with suspicion. I'd almost become accustomed to this and still there was something in me responding to the expectation that I ought to explain myself to the corporal if I could, but as the corporal's face conveyed that I was not only a mystery hardly worth the trouble, I was also a contagion of some kind, I veered between feelings of "fuck you" and the temptation to identify myself as a human citizen of some unknown worth.

What I assumed about the Corporal's life, what I'd heard and gathered from what he was not inclined to keep secret, when he spoke to Sergeant Russell and I stood close by awaiting my next order, was that in spite of seventeen years in the army the corporal had never been in combat. Corporal Bickford lowered his voice and said that he wanted to think of himself as a soldier and yet, he had doubts. Sergeant Russell assured Corporal Bickford that the shit was bound to hit the fan again; the Reds were certain to cross the 38th Parallel and the corporal could count on being in the thick of it. As far as the sergeant was concerned he'd be "long gone, retired." He had hoped, he repeated to the corporal, to be a thirty-year man, but the traitor from Missouri, that he'd actually voted for, ruined it all. The corporal laughed and said that he hoped the sergeant didn't hold it against him that he came from Missouri. The sergeant smiled and reminded the corporal that the corporal's tending his sergeant's hangovers had prevented or at least curtailed the corporal's drinking, forestalling the trouble that would result in the corporal's being busted again; to say nothing of the booze that would darken Corporal Bickford's Injun red complexion so that no one would ever take him for a white man. They laughed. Sergeant Russell again cursed, "Harry the traitor."

I'd misunderstood. On the way to chow and on the way to the library, in the library, as my attention drifted from *The Sound and the Fury*, I realized how I'd misunderstood Sergeant Russell's grievance. The "Harry" he'd first referred to when he spoke of betrayal I'd assumed as a correspondent in an adulterous affair with his wife. But the sergeant was not divorcing his wife; he was divorcing the great love of his life, the Army. And it was former president Harry Truman, a man the sergeant had trusted, as Harry too, the sergeant claimed, had once been a member of the Klu Klux Klan; and yet it was Truman, the former Commander-in-Chief who gave the order for the mongrelization of the army, surrendering the military and society to miscegenation, and the rule of chaos. Corporal Bickford said that it was NCOs like Sergeant Russell who made the Army work. Sergeant Russell shrugged and said that he couldn't be persuaded to reenlist. He calculated the benefits he would receive as a retiree after twenty rather than thirty years, and said he'd live reasonably well. He hoped his papers were processed promptly so that he could be on his way by the end of the month, "Before Captain Jefferson the new CO, a colored, assumes command." Corporal Bickford commiserated. He apologized for the former president since he too came from Missouri, but the corporal said in his own behalf he hadn't voted for Truman. And the corporal glanced at me as someone who was complicit in Truman's rise to power.

I'd seen that look of recognition flash in the corporal's eyes before. Corporal Bickford was billeted in the same barracks where on weekends I visited Bruce and Gabe with my record collection of the Norman Granz's jazz concerts. Gabe's military occupational specialty named him a cook, and he did make meals at the Mess Hall palatable. Gabe was also an aspiring musician/composer and he played trumpet, piano, bass, and guitar. I'd heard Gabe on guitar; he was wonderful. Bruce who worked at the Quartermaster claimed that he had played alto saxophone until he'd heard Charlie Parker and gave it up. Now his ambition, once he completed his three-year tour of duty, was to become an entrepreneur of the new music, to help make it known all over the world.

In the blessed corner of the barracks, the portable phonograph on the floor, we listened. There wasn't much talk. Sometimes there was discussion and Gabe and Bruce could articulate something about the music they wanted a greater understanding of, Bruce demonstrating an aspect of his question by scat singing. I throbbed on the periphery. I'd confessed to Gabe that the music we listened to had provoked an impossible dream of fluency from which I'd never escape. Bruce smiled and said, "Yes." He quoted a composer whose name I've forgotten and said to me, "Music expresses what can't be expressed in any other way."

The evening Corporal Bickford passed by our corner on his way out of the barracks and paused, staring for a moment, we were listening to Thelonious Monk. Gabe played an invisible piano in accompaniment. We laughed as helplessly, as mercilessly as children hearing the endless innovation that beggared the word lyricism. Listening to Monk I laughed, trembled, heard a song being discovered again and again in every note, songs inside the song, music inside the music. As the music moved and shook us and I felt a nakedness, my eyes rolling in my head, I had a notion of the devout and frenzied prayer my father had fled on his way to Marxism. My laughter, Bruce's laughter, Gabriel's laughter hadn't been meant as mockery. Corporal Bickford had stopped for a moment and watched us. My eyes swept his face, Bruce and Gabe also looking in his direction, the laughter that shook us inside out wasn't meant as a vindication, or celebration of the arrival of the new company commander who was approximately of the same dark hue as Gabe and Bruce, and the corporal certain we were laughing at him and that I was in league with something indeed dark, and I couldn't think of any way to explain, even if I could have caught my breath; and I couldn't defend myself without compromising my dream of creating something beautiful, and that now seemed possible—at the very least I knew the aspiration to be inexhaustible.

After pay day, on Saturday nights, once a month, I sat alone in the enlisted men's club, drank and preached temperance to myself. My silent exhortation like the other languid thoughts journeying through my mind, each thought having the authority of magic, carried the danger of an imperative I had to obey, this sensuous mental life a seduction I couldn't resist. I don't know whether my preaching moderation was responsible for keeping the binge a once a month occasion that became a fortnightly necessity years later, but I also felt a great democratic surge, a powerful urge toward universality, and when I got into a couple of scraps, the cause of which I never remembered, I did remember a joyousness that lingered even the morning after. I could find as a solitary drinker a larger embrace of humanity.

The windows that ran around the enlisted men's club filled with the bay of Inchon, ocean, clouds, sky of stars and riding moon swirling like the rings of Saturn, as inside, at the center I journeyed an otherness that almost made me a regular guy, comprehensible to the others. The morning after, days after I would hear theories about the cause of the scraps I'd been in and I didn't know which to credit; but I was happy, and the theorists offering explanation seemed happy too. But there were also in those nights moments when I was a kid again, and I knew how one cowardly act can require numberless acts of bravery as I saw myself again leaping from roof to roof.

Sergeant Russell's papers came through. He would be shipping out, stateside, within a week. The remaining days were filled with awkward farewells. Various troopers came up to Sergeant Russell, clutched him, shoved him, Sergeant Russell clutched and shoved back; they shook hands and thumped one another on the back. Sergeant Russell's repeated farewells to Corporal Bickford cautioned that now that the corporal was no longer charged with ministering to the sergeant's hangovers the corporal might be tempted to pick up a drink, in which case the corporal was likely to capsize his life, lose a stripe, possibly find himself in the stockade; and the sergeant said it would behoove the corporal to find a new standard operational procedure for his duties to keep him on track and away from trouble; for Corporal Bickford said Sergeant Russell, "There wasn't anything so bad that a drink wouldn't make it worse."

Master Sergeant Keating would assume responsibility of the Motor Pool under the aegis of First Lieutenant Flood. Sergeant Keating was a short round man with a permanent air of preoccupation. He loved nothing so much as the automobile engine. People were interesting in so far as analogy might compare them with the workings of the engine. When Sergeant Keating walked across the Motor Pool floor on his way to confer with Sergeant Russell and Corporal Bickford his hands reached out to touch affectionately the fender of a Jeep, the hood of a truck.

Sergeant Keating's misgiving concerning Mr. Kim's clairvoyance in locating a malfunction in a vehicle engine persisted quite aside from Mr. Kim's record of accuracy. It was, for Sergeant Keating, the process he objected to, some sort of magic, intuition given as dark largesse to be paid for later with malaise, one's soul losing some portion of light. The only thing that would do was the moral and step by step labor to diagnose and correct the malady as thoroughly as possible, fondling and studying each part of the machine with the care of a lover discovering the mystery for the first time. What was scientific was humble, constant labor, prayer.

Sergeant Russell and Corporal Bickford discussed Mr. Kim and me as I stood close by. Sergeant Russell had reassured Sergeant Keating that we were anomalies he needn't worry himself about. Sergeant Russell spoke softly. Corporal Bickford raised his voice, glanced in my direction and said, "a numbnuts fuck up." Sergeant Russell said, "Naw, more like an old hound goin' deaf, he ain't entirely bad." I said, "I heard that." Sergeant Russell and Corporal Bickford laughed and applauded, as if my response were proof of some remedial progress achieved by my proximity to them. Sergeant Keating studied me with a look of resignation, I was something he'd never be able to fix, and he didn't want to waste his time trying to figure out how.

Mr. Kim loaded the metal cabinet that was part of Sergeant Russell's office onto his back, bending low, lifting his chin so that he could see where he was going and went off to deliver it as directed to headquarters. When I moved to assist Mr. Kim, Sergeant Russell commanded, "As you were, trooper, don't interfere with the man's job of work."

Mr. Kim wore an L-shaped frame on his back and had ropes that lashed the metal cabinet to the frame, the ropes tied at the center of Mr. Kim's chest, he grasped the ends of the rope. Bent forward the cabinet jutted out a couple of feet past the top of his head. He made his way forward across the littered floor. I thought I saw Mr. Kim limping. His progress across the floor strewn with barrels, tires, tools and the carcasses of two vehicles awaiting resurrection made Mr. Kim's movement herky-jerky, like a man precariously traversing a tight rope, about to topple any moment. Mr. Kim's right foot trembled in air and sweat ran down his impassive face. I followed him across the floor; I would catch him if he fell. The two sergeants and the corporal laughed as the gravitational force of Mr. Kim's labor pulled me in his wake.

Mr. Kim made his way through the Motor Pool into the shed where the worn and spare tires were stocked and where the Korean workers took their meals; the GIs complained that they couldn't stand the stench of kim chi, a spicy dish consisting of pickled cabbage, peppers and garlic; the troopers claimed that the stink, like the rank smell of the honey buckets of human shit that the Koreans hauled to fertilize their rice paddies, made them ill. In the shed Mr. Sung came up alongside me, bowed slightly touching my elbow so lightly that if I hadn't seen him I wouldn't have felt his touch. "Please" he whispered. He clasped his hands at the center of his chest, lifted his head and gestured toward his throat where a crucifix hung. "I am new Christian" he said, "almost one year." I said, "Yes." He said, smiling," I see you study Mr. Kim, good for you, Mr. Kim number one." I turned losing sight of Mr. Kim who had progressed out of the shed. When I turned back to Mr. Sung I saw that he had again picked up the broom that was almost always in his hands. Mr. Sung, a thin man, perhaps in his thirties, seemed to sweep incessantly, the broom might have had some force of its own which propelled him into peripatetic circles around the floor as he spoke. Mr. Sung's face bore an astonishing resemblance to Buster Keaton's, although the droll melancholy of the Keaton face was more than mitigated by Mr. Sung's mobilizing his cheeks, mouth, and eyes into the appearance of happiness. He swept in a circle around me that grew wider, accompanied by smiles and bows, but I was kept within the center of his orbit.

The other Korean worker, Mr. Shin, had finished eating. He was young, handsome, powerfully built, and his habitual silence seemed a means of keeping his anger in check. I found it unnerving to look directly into his eyes. I'd learned that he could speak English, but rarely did; when he had to speak, he spoke in Korean to Mr. Sung or Mr. Kim. He'd finished eating and was looking down a well of stacked truck tires, speaking frugally, his silences longer than anything he articulated out loud. He spoke in Korean into the well of tires and Mr. Sung answered in Korean. At one point Mr. Shin said in English, "My rice bowl." Mr. Sung nodded.

After a time I began to understand. Mr. Sung and Mr. Shin were concerned with losing their positions. They knew of the change in command and didn't know what it would mean for them. Mr. Sung finally asked if I would speak in their behalf. I said that I would and tried to explain that I lacked the authority to determine the outcome; and I doubted that the changes in the chain of command would affect them. I think Mr. Sung interpreted my statement as a reluctance to speak in their behalf. Before I could reassure him he invoked the name of Mr. Kim. "Mr. Kim's words are spoken to persons of all ranks from his heart to the hearts of all." Mr. Sung paused momentarily with the broom for emphasis. He looked at me, took my silence for acknowledgment, resumed sweeping and said, "Mr.

Kim is householder who supports much family and any who arrive in our village and claim to be family."

Mr. Sung swept, his footwork exceptional. The volume of the circle was commodious. The diameter constant, he and his broom always in front of me. I repeated that he was not to worry, I would speak in his and the others' behalf, and that it was doubtful that they would lose their positions. I danced to the right circling out of his orbit. Mr. Sung called after me in his sweet, importuning voice and said that Mr. Kim never acted out of a desire for gain, even spiritual, and Mr. Kim had told him that the world of nirvana and samsara are one.

On Sergeant Russell's last day his eyes shone with a benevolent light, the cigarette smoke he exhaled had the odor of bourbon, he stood ramrod straight in his freshly pressed and clean khakis supervising the installation of Sergeant Keating. First Lieutenant Flood would eventually appear at the Motor pool, look about as though his most fleeting glance gathered all and everything into his vision, and unless Sergeant Keating communicated some problem, say "Good work soldier, carry on," and return to his life at the Officer's Club. Sergeant Russell continued to whisper cautionary advice into Corporal Bickford's ear. Mr. Kim had removed Sergeant Russell's desk and chair. He set up a seat for Sergeant Keating, instigated and insisted upon by Sergeant Russell, that was a sort of throne, a pillowed bench and back support atop of a four sided ladder structure, almost a story high, the kind of pinnacle from which a lifeguard could peer out into the sea and study the waves for signs of those drowning. Mr. Kim had also fetched for Sergeant Keating, (and it was Sergeant Russell who knew where these items were to be found) a pair of binoculars and a bullhorn. Sergeant Keating ensconced on the top of what in the distance could appear as the skeletal structure of a light house looked through his binoculars across the distance, placed the binoculars in his lap, brought the bull-horn to his lips, and in a voice like God thundering the announcement of the Flood to Noah, leaves and birds blown from the soon to be drowned trees, howled, "Kominsky you dumb shit, check the spark plugs."

When Mr. Kim returned to Sergeant Russell to see if anything more was required of him in setting up Sergeant Keating's place of command, I saw that Mr. Kim's limp was pronounced. He locomoted forward bobbing up and down, the heel of his right foot touching the floor gingerly, he maintained his balance. He came to rest and waited for his next order. I looked down at the hurt foot that gave off an odor like meat going bad. The foot was wrapped in clean white cloth, soaked in some kind of disinfectant not strong enough to obscure the smell of the injury. Mr. Kim wore, as did the other Korean workers, rubber slippers the GIs called "E.T.-WA" boots, which was pidgin Korean that translated for the GIs and Koreans into "Come On Boots"—or "Hurry Up Boots" depending on the tone of the voice.

Mr. Kim stood still, waiting. His body like a ballet dancer of unfathomable and seemingly fragile grace kept the secret of its enormous strength from the eye in the smooth, unmuscular lines of a pre-adolescent boy. His head was something else.

Somewhere between old and eternal it might have been hewn from stone. And his hands too, the left one with the four missing fingers, hands as brutalized as the unexpurgated history of the world. From the epicanthic folds his dark eyes obtruded, he resembled someone afflicted with a thyroid condition.

Sergeants Russell and Keating and Corporal Bickford stood together holding their noses. Corporal Bickford said something about the Koreans disobeying orders and eating lunch in the work area. They laughed. Mr. Kim studied the men working and loafing, the two sergeants and the corporal clinking glasses and toasting, and beyond the roar of all the noise and the babble of the celebratory expletives he seemed to see into the heart of time.

On Sergeant Russell's last day the farewells, the various toasts with beer and bourbon, a greater disorder prevailed, work and party co-existing in a rowdiness that buried the feelings a man found inconvenient.

I said to Sergeant Russell, "Mr. Kim's foot is seriously injured, he needs immediate medical attention." Sergeant Russell looked at me with a glazed, benevolent stare. I repeated myself to Sergeant Keating, and Corporal Bickford. Mr. Kim watched, the event interesting in itself, he and his foot only incidentally involved in a circumstance, the solution to which might be manifest after eons of reincarnation. Resting on one of the lower steps of Sergeant Keating's tower was the bullhorn. I picked it up, put it to my lips and aimed in the direction of Sergeant Russell, Sergeant Keating, and Corporal Bickford, and yelled, "Mr. Kim's foot is injured, we must get him to the medics!" The pronouncement boomed, and pervaded every iota of space, echoing in the vast metal, high ceiling structure of the Motor Pool; the command repeated itself.

Mr. Kim and I, with a resentful PFC Glidding at the wheel of the Jeep, since neither Mr. Kim nor I could drive, were dispatched by Sergeant Russell, Sergeant Keating and Corporal Bickford, and many of the cheering men, the Jeep regarded as a ship of fools off on a journey that Sergeant Keating and Corporal Bickford wished could be interminable, Sergeant Russell smiling beatifically since he no longer had a care.

It was a hazy, humid day in early August. The jeep without a canopy moved in clouds of dust. Mr. Kim, PFC Glidding and I, coated and grained like relics, bounced and squinted. To my left through the haze and dust I could make out the forms of the Mama-sans following the receding ocean, bending to retrieve what the retreating sea revealed. The spectral shapes of the women, filling the cone shaped baskets tied around their waists, shadowed the ocean that withdrew toward the horizon, where the low lying clouds marked the place where the ocean would disappear.

Mr. Kim, slate gray and as textured as a statue, seemed to be enjoying the ride. His eyes flickered beneath his stone brow: he rocked, and I became mesmerized watching his swaying back and forth. There was the slightest hint of a smile in the curvature of his mouth, and his foot gave off a mortal stink. I had one eye closed and squinted through the other between the splayed fingers of my right hand, which I held across my face. PFC Glidding sitting up front, alone, drove and cursed.

Keeping my fingers latticed over my open eye I turned to watch the ocean uncover itself on the way to disappearing as the indefatigable shadows of women rummaged in the mud for edibles and kelp.

PFC Glidding gripped the wheel and sped the jeep down the rucked road, the great cowl of dust accompanying us all the way, the rushing road consumed and never ending, he muttered to himself or someone or something the injustices inflicted on him. He repeated it all over and over again; he shouted, the better to hear it, to make sure he wasn't forgetting anything.

Each month he sent his allotment check home to his mother, which she accepted as her due, without ever a word of appreciation. He had never done anything that his father found praiseworthy, and all the family's resources, including what he sent each month had gone into funding the lavish wedding for his older sister Gladys, then her divorce, and now Glady's training in the college of cosmetology; and Gladys was no more inclined to acknowledge his contribution than his parents. All of this history culminated in the injustice Seargeant Russell imposed on him. He, Private First Class Glidding tainted because I had once laid hands on him, bloodied his lip, and now here he was ordered to chauffeur "a gook and a misfit."

At the Motor Pool, when he had protested, not able to stop, repeating himself, he interrupted and continued to complain to Sgt. Russell whose booze-fueled serenity had been breached for a half a moment, long enough for the Sergeant's glacial eyes to light up as he said, " PFC Glidding, I promise, if you don't shut the fuck up I'm gonna take you by the windpipe and you'll find out if you can breathe through your asshole."

In the careening jeep PFC Glidding had recapitulated his inventory of injustices, never certain that he hadn't forgotten something important, he shuffled the inventory in a cyclical recitation that had no end until we arrived in front of the Quonset hut that was the medical center; he slammed his foot on the brake, we lurched, bounced, almost launched out of the jeep. Glidding hung on to the wheel, bug-eyed and loony with revelation. Mr. Kim and I climbed out of the jeep. "Glidding," I said, "We'll see you when we come out." He smiled, overcome, rested his arms against the steering wheel and laid his head on his arms. Encased in grit he too appeared a piece of statuary with incongruous human eyes.

At the side of the door was a spigot of water and beneath it a bucket. I turned on the tap. Mr. Kim and I attempted to wash the dirt from our faces and necks. We beat storms of dust from one another's chest, backs, slapped at our trousers. He bowed after I thumped clouds of dust from his chest and back, and I bowed to him after he did the same for me. We attempted to rinse our swampy heads.

Inside, the staff sergeant stood with a hypodermic syringe in his raised right hand at the center of some eight GIs seated in two rows on metal folding chairs. A few were smirking. The bald, stout sergeant, built wide and close to the ground, cheerful and grim, spoke in the voice of command that is made and perfected in the realm where sergeants are made: his right cheek, ballooned with chewing tobacco, jiggled; "Mens!" he barked," you had to play, and now you pay; however, you sorry assed bastards who' been warned but went to Chancre Alley anyway, well I'll stick you with a needle, but they's got shit there the docs ain't even catalogued. You better start thinkin' about how you're gonna say goodbye to your wives and sweethearts back home. Before you go deaf and blind you can take your Tough Shit forms to the chaplain for advice." The men stirred in the metal folding chairs, several laughed. The sergeant gripped the hypodermic like a dagger he was about to plunge into the chest of the trooper seated closest to him. The boy jumped from his chair, fell on his ass and looked up stupidly. The sergeant hollered, "You think I'm here for your entertainment! When I yell Ten Hut I wanna hear your pussies pucker! 'Ten Hut!" All but the trooper seated on the floor struggling to rise and one very young trooper whose face had been stamped with a defiance made by everything that is not supposed to happen to a child—still hung over, he rose like a snake being charmed out of a basket, and all the others snapped to attention.

Standing they looked like figures mined from a grotto, patinated in grime, sweat etching human lips and eyes in their faces, the sergeant's voice an anvil compounding an impossible-to-follow incantation of curses, polymorphous, enraged, the foul tirade seemed to pound the troopers into being on the spot. "And you filthy sons-a-bitches march your candy asses outta here and clean yourselves up. Try to look like soldiers. Then I'll stick you with medicine."

They trooped outside. I heard water running from the tap. The sergeant looked at me, nearly saw me but I gained obscurity from standing next to Mr. Kim. The sergeant turned away spitting out residual curses, clearing his throat, the puffed cheek throbbing under his mad eye, a thread of tobacco juice drooled on his chin. The sergeant's thumb dabbed at his chin, flecked and endowed the air, a master finessing chiaroscuro in a vision only he could see.

In an undertone he chanted at the screen door that slammed shut behind the trooper's filing out; "You shudda stayed home, but you left, right, left, right…."

Again I explained to the sergeant why I was there. I don't know what he heard. Briefly the cheek puffed with chewing tobacco paused, the sergeant still, concentrating; the ballooned cheek wobbled again and the sergeant repeated, "What are you standin' there for? You think you got something special?" For the third time I explained that I wasn't on sick call because I had a dose. That I might be claiming a malady that wasn't VD irritated him; a trooper coming on sick call with something he couldn't treat was a provocation. I said it all again in a soothing voice. The sergeant growled, "The Doc, Captain Martin ain't here, he had to haul ass to Seoul, a meeting' with the big brass. Come back tomorra.'" I pointed to Mr. Kim's foot; I said, "You can smell it, I hope it's not gangrene. He needs a shot of antibiotic and to get the injury cleaned up." "I tole you," the sergeant said, "I ain't authorized for that, and the gook ain't authorized personnel." "Mr. Kim works for us at the Motor Pool, at least give him a shot." The sergeant, in a state of disbelief because I was still standing there, arguing with him, looked from me to Mr. Kim. Mr. Kim stood still and watched. The raving sergeant might have been turbulent weather that Mr. Kim studied through a window. "Private you can try tomorra', when the captain is here, now haul ass!" I said, "Please." The staff sergeant's white-hot face thrust close to mine. "There's a gook Red Cross station about a mile up the hill, now you and this kim chi-eatin'-piss-complexioned-dwarf double time outta here, or you're gonna need medical attention."

We walked. My strolling, Mr. Kim's leisurely limp taunting the sergeant, I could feel his heat on my neck. At the door I turned to say "fuck you sergeant" and Mr. Kim shook his head no. I kept silent and the sergeant and I exchanged looks of such pure hatred that I felt exhilarated, oddly free.

I looked around. The jeep and PFC Glidding were nowhere in sight. Up the road in a swirl of dust I saw the back end of a bus, one of our two and a half ton trucks heading back across the causeway to the base. Now I was close to raving, but in the presence of Mr. Kim I restrained myself. He pointed in the opposite direction. "That way. We walk, not far. Maybe catch ride." Mr. Kim's limp was nimble. His seesaw motion propelled him forward at a quick march pace. I was not inclined to question his intention to walk to the Red Cross station. When I imagined the ordeals of his life, compared to the privilege of mine, I couldn't assess what might be an ordinary task for him, and what might constitute suffering, and I felt the need to defer to him. I followed Mr. Kim up the road toward the hills that climbed into the mountains. A small dog dashed by my ankles; I was sure I had seen it, and it seemed to me a promising omen that the mutt hadn't already disappeared into some hungry family's cooking pot.

I followed Mr. Kim's hip-hop ascent up the road. I thought that we had probably walked a mile; no one passed us and there wasn't any sign of the Red Cross station.

The heat had sweated the color out of the mountain, shrubs and rocks moon gray, the sun's heavy light pouring down, the color of pewter. The gradual climb required an effort to continue at a steady pace, at least for me. Up ahead, about fifty yards, Mr. Kim, with the peculiar gait of a three-legged goat, made his way without pause.

When I was fairly certain that we must have walked at least two miles, perhaps three, I decided that I would ask Mr. Kim after we continued a while longer if he had any idea where we were. He continued on ceaselessly and I was ashamed to ask him to stop and rest for my sake. I wanted to make my inquiry after an honorable length of time.

The road was too narrow for trucks, perhaps a jeep could negotiate the road but its progress wouldn't have been that much faster than traveling on foot. The road could accommodate the small powerful Manchurian ponies and carts we hadn't yet passed. I wondered why the Red Cross would set up an aid station in so difficult a place to get to, but maybe the inhabitants we hadn't seen could get to the place on foot or hauled in a cart by one of the ponies.

We came to a turn in the road where there were two paths, one an undulating descent and the other veering off to the right that ascended. Mr. Kim waited for me. When I came alongside him he said, “That way,” pointing to the ascending path. “Not too far. You okay GI?” I nodded yes and we continued.

Alongside the rock strewn path there was some shrubbery spawning in the inhospitable geologic strata, bordering the road the rocks imbedded in the ground were covered with green fungus-like stuff.

I began to think of the hike as an exercise in silence, saying only what it was absolutely necessary to say. My initial fatigue had passed and I made my way at an even pace although the crushed rock underfoot required staying alert, my ankles wobbled; there wasn’t any place where the ground was level.

I was thirsty. It hadn’t seemed necessary at the outset to carry a canteen with water. Neither did I have a watch, but looking down into the bay I could see that the tide was in, the smoking glare of the sun had inched toward the west, and remembering recent maneuvers, (although nothing really felt recent, everything had become remote, something dubiously remembered under the dominion of this journey, declaring its own ethos which I tried to understand). I did recall maneuvers on similar terrain, with full pack and M-1 rifle when troops covered about two miles an hour, and given the tension behind my knees I estimated that we had probably been walking, climbing up and down for about three hours.

The hot breeze on my face ceased and became moist weight on my shoulders. Mr. Kim ahead and below me disappeared behind a great shelf of rock. The claw of a stillborn, leafless tree jutted out of the rock, each talon of branch against the sky pointing in a contradictory direction. I called out to Mr. Kim, "Where are we?" If I wasn't able to keep up with Mr. Kim I'd be lost in boundlessness.

I skidded down an incline into a path that was a little wider and more level. Some twenty paces ahead of me stood an old man, lean as a stick, his pony hitched to a wooden cart. The smell of human shit in lidded buckets tied with rope and packed tightly in the cart had preceded the sight of the old man, and his toothless smile. His white beard, the threads of a spider's web, through which I could see the bony lump of his Adam's apple rode up and down to the faint sound of his breath, whistling through his nose; on his head a hat like a sawed off stove pipe with a wide black brim; his white blouse and trousers resembled pajamas. He and Mr. Kim were talking. The small, broad, Manchurian pony stood harnessed to the cart.

Beyond the stink of the shit, the conversation between the old man and Mr. Kim in Korean went on and on, and I couldn't guess from the sound if the discussion was coming to a conclusion. The monumental head of the pony appeared composed of flies out of which looked the most humane eyes I'd ever seen in any creature. The pox of flies swarmed and buzzed around the pony's head. I looked into the immense eyes of the pony and waited.

The farewell went on and on; they were inordinately grateful for having met and although I couldn't understand a word I thought I heard some parting phrase repeated over and over, and watched a long series of ritual bows. Again and again they seemed at the point of parting but resumed the repetition of the same phrase and commenced another series of bows.

The old man on foot, the Manchurian pony hauling the cart of honey buckets, a stream of flies hovering above them, they descended the path in the direction we had come. The smell lingered when they were no longer in sight. I turned and saw Mr. Kim sitting on the ground, his legs sprawled in front of him. I don't remember a discussion. The accord was present in my mind and I took Mr. Kim on my back. I bent low and helped hoist his thighs up over my shoulders, he held the sides of my head with the palms of his hands and sat up straight, his bottom centered on the back of my neck and spread out across my shoulders. His legs dangled past my waist and the odor of his injured foot rose to my nostrils. His weight didn't feel like too much. Still I was anxious. Perched on me, Mr. Kim pointed to the ascending path. The failure to transport Mr. Kim could be damning in some way I didn't want to imagine. I assumed from the dialogue I hadn't understood that the old man had reassured Mr. Kim, confirmed that our destination existed.

Hiking up and down in a laborious circle, a kind of slow grinding roller coaster ascent and descent over narrow paths terraced into a labyrinth, I made my way and Mr. Kim on and above me made encouraging sounds. We came out onto a plateau. I could see the bay, the roofs of the Quonset huts that made up the base, and the causeway (that I'd heard had been built by American POW's during World War II) that crossed the bay to the entrance of the base. Looking down I had the impression that I hadn't climbed higher than the tenement roof I'd climbed as a boy in search of a breeze, during a stifling New York summer.

The stones churned beneath my feet, Mr. Kim gained weight, and as I trod the inconclusive journey my anxieties were honed into imponderables; what if Mr. Kim on my back was the weight of my shortcomings—lacks, the palpable moral weakness which I struggled under and if I unloaded the weight I would lose even the truth of this, and live a weakling's life of illusion.

I was thirsty. My thighs were beginning to cramp. I paused for a moment. Mr. Kim's arm extended in front of my face, the hand with only the thumb remaining pointed to a horizon of mountains where the sky and the earth were separated by the thinnest white line of cloud. Was there something he wanted me to understand from the vision he pointed to? Softly Mr. Kim knocked on the top of my head with his knuckles and I plodded on. I was parched; my temples throbbed. My knees and back felt stiff, my hamstrings were taut and I was afraid that if I stopped to rest I wouldn't be able to go on. I believed that Mr. Kim thought so too, or he would have suggested a rest.

I stumbled, glanced upward and saw Mr. Kim extend his arms like wings, aiding me in correcting my balance. It wasn't just exhaustion, I'd marched beyond that, or even the assortment of aches in my back and legs that promised more interesting pain tomorrow, but now I was walking with a slight limp; Mr. Kim was part of my back, like a hunchback's hump, the deformity of weight belonged to me and what I resented was the burning on the back of my right heel, probably a blister.

My boots had never fit properly. I knew it would be futile to go to the quartermaster to exchange them for a pair that might fit. The quartermaster would only hand me another set of boots that would be too large or too small. I should have returned to Mama-san in the black market. She was usually better stocked than the quartermaster, and she was patient. Although Mama-san would try to sell me scotch, cigarettes, cans of Spam, and a virgin of dubious provenance she kept in shadow behind a gauzy curtain. That I had elected, by default, to live with the discomfort of the ill-fitting boots rather than return to Mama-san suggested another flaw in my character. The burning on the back of my right heel retribution for my procrastination.

My side ached somewhere in the region of my kidney, I no longer thought anything, sometime in some past I had reckoned that certainly we were lost and given the tint of the sky suggesting the end of day, the refinements of my pain, compared to the more orderly forced marches on maneuvers, I'd estimated that I'd hiked about eight or nine miles, and that if I'd have been on hard, level blacktop instead of the infernal and constant climbing up and down I'd have covered twice the distance. But now exhaustion blanked out all speculation, what I saw, I saw impressionalistically, images in fragments whose implication of thought lasted no longer than the next labored breath. At one point I turned my head, looked up, and had the impression that the faint moon sat on Mr. Kim's head in a sea of sky where the sun still reigned leaking twilight, becoming night at the edges. Ahead of me I saw earth and sky transfigured into a horizon like a great curtain of simmering water, and I felt I could walk through the curtain to the edge of the world and fall off.

In the near distance I saw something hoped for, unsure I'd actually seen it, a small stone, whitewashed dwelling with a tin roof mirroring a darkened sky rushing toward oblivion. There was a red cross painted on the white door. A figure in a white smock flashed in a window and then I saw nothing. I tottered. Mr. Kim put his hands over my eyes and I halted. I felt him climb down, the separation, the sudden lightness disorienting, some part of me falling away, amputated. He was standing in front of me repeating something solicitous and urgent, "No more carry"; and the hand with the four stumps and the thumb waved in front of my face blocking my sight of the window where I thought I'd seen a figure appear. "No," said Mr. Kim, "you are soldier, must not lose face, not . . ." and his hands described a beast of burden, and we limped toward the white house.

Doctor Park, the physician in attendance at the Red Cross station, knew Mr. Kim. The young doctor's greeting conveyed the impression that he'd been waiting for me to arrive. Mr. Kim said something in Korean. I, overcome and grateful for having reached a destination that existed, praised the immaculate facility and the view of mountains from the window. Doctor Park smiled at the unaccountable good fortune of the beautiful view. The young doctor and I, circumspect and in a tizzy, went on smiling and gaping at one another, and I felt an embrace although we never touched. Doctor Park was deferential to Mr. Kim, and looked toward him for approval as he translated, as if Mr. Kim had the capacity to read the hieroglyphics of gestures and facial tics that revealed the gist of all languages. The more precise translation offered to me was a courtesy. Doctor Park said that Mr. Kim apologized for taking me on such a roundabout journey. Mr. Kim knew where and approximately when he was likely to encounter his old friend on the road, and his old friend was to arrange for his niece to serve as a wet nurse for a baby born in Mr. Kim's village who was of mixed race. None of the women in Mr. Kim's village were willing to nurse the baby, and the mother, formally employed in one of Inchon's bars, had disappeared.

Doctor Park said he would attend to Mr. Kim's foot. However, he didn't have any penicillin left and asked if I'd be good enough to contribute to the purchase of some more. I emptied my pockets. He emptied his. He chose only American dollars and explained that there was a rumor that the military was about to change the appearance of military pay currency and there was a panic in the Black Market, only dollars were acceptable. Doctor Park dispatched a young boy to run the errand to the nearby Chinese ghetto where there was certain to be an ample supply of antibiotic. Mr. Kim stood on one foot with his eyes closed.

LA OVERTIME

I FOUGHT OFF SLEEP FOR A YEAR. The noise of the train was terrific, the textbooks slipped from my lap, the lights in the subway car blinked on and off. I sat, a stranger pressed to my side, and my cheek rested on the window where lightning flashed making the tunnel vivid for an instant. Thunder boomed in the intervals of dark. Almost drowsing or nearly awake I'd started to reach for the text that had fallen to the floor, but Professor Kleiner's droning voice found its way into my sleep and emphasized what he'd been emphasizing in class; and it was unclear whether he repeated himself because he thought the review was essential or he'd forgotten that he'd said all this, exactly the same way, on the two previous nights. "The common sense notion of time in which events take place in succession interprets time as something moving toward the future. However, Parmenides insisted that change and becoming were illusions, and Heraclitus asserted that there was no permanence, that change characterized everything. But according to Newton, time was independent of and prior to events; still Leibniz argued that there can be no time independent of events, time is formed by events."

The grinding shriek of the train wheels, my head bouncing off the window and the shock of light peeling my eyes open, I accepted the textbook the stranger had picked up from the floor and nodded thanks. I stumbled to the train doors, others moving to the doors bumped and crowded against me.

After work at American Mills warehouse I'd descended into the subway for the ride uptown to City College, as I did every evening from Monday to Thursday. I would have to change trains at 59th Street. On the first part of the trip, caught in the crush of rush hour, I stood hanging on to a strap overhead and dozed. My body was shoved toward the train doors at a stop that wasn't mine. I grasped a pole and resisted the tide, the image of Reiko flared again, intruding light that made me blink and this time I followed the young woman carrying the portfolio and books. The grace of her movement was reminiscent. I let the crowd of bodies move me out onto the station platform. I wanted to follow the woman, wanted to come alongside her to confirm that it wasn't Reiko. I knew it wasn't, but I had to see. Once before I'd encountered the figure with the black hair hanging down to her waist. I needed to deny or affirm what seemed familiar, known to me in some intimate way. The crowd of bodies around me thinned out, people rushing off in different directions. The sounds of trains screeched and rumbled. From a concession, next to a flight of steps that was an exit leading up to the street came the aroma of frying potatoes and onions. I hadn't had time for supper but I couldn't stop for a hot dog and fries without losing sight of the young woman who had picked up her pace. Lost in the strange city that was home to me I had a vague recollection of a ravishment that was prerequisite to learning something, and I followed the young woman up the steps to the street. The signs on the subway walls with arrows pointing in different directions and names of streets said that I was somewhere in the South Bronx.

It was dark. She was walking at a brisk pace. If I called to her to say I wasn't a menace she'd be alarmed, given the night and the city; I considered, but couldn't stop. She turned a corner.

The lights in the apartment house windows lit up, warmer than the first stars turning on in the city sky. She paused ahead of me and switched the portfolio and books from one arm to the other. I came closer. Across the street in front of a neon-lit bodega, next to a closed and gated check cashing place stood a group of laughing young men. "Please," I called at her back. From across the street one of the young men yelled, "Guitarra!" another yelled joyously, "Mami." Another shouted something in Spanish. She shouted back something in Spanish that sounded angry. There was some shoving across the street. One young man clinched the arms of another, while a third edged himself between the two. A fourth remained in the doorway, his hands in his pockets, watching. The one lounging in the doorway raised his voice and called across the street in English, "Blessed be the womb that carried you into this world."

The beauty who was not Reiko sized me up and turned to the three young men strutting to the curb. All three wore pork pie hats with the brims turned up; the hats were green, crimson, and gold. Their three-quarter length black leather jackets were belted though the night was mild and they all smiled. One stepped up on the curb, looked at me, and asked, "Is he bothering you?" She said, "No." Then they talked for a while in Spanish. The one who asked if I was bothering her said in English, "You sure?" She said, "Yes." He said, "Okay." The three turned and walked back across the street. The one in the doorway across the street cried out, "Adios mi vida."

She said, "I just saved your life. You can carry my books." I walked alongside her, carried her books, and tried not to stare. She was accustomed to negotiating male attention and her means was an aspect of her imagination, which was focused on something else. Scraps of music blared from a window and faded. A car cruised by and a young man hanging out the passenger's side window screamed a tribute at her. His voice faded. We walked beyond the sounds of traffic into a muted street of brownstones, eavesdropping on the sounds of our footsteps. I wanted to say something, fill the silence, but I couldn't. If I tried to explain it would sound weird; I didn't understand myself, although I was no longer concerned with frightening her. She was not one who could be easily frightened. Still I thought it would be a mistake to declare that I didn't want her to disappear from my life, and I couldn't think of a thing to say, since what I needed to say felt momentous. She said, "You're lost." I said, "Yes." "You don't live in the Bronx." I nodded yes. "You've followed me before?" "Only once," I said, "I'm sorry, I couldn't think of a way to introduce myself." "Oh," she said, and laughed. I was glad she laughed. "Well," I found myself saying, "the truth sounds like a lie, the usual thing, you remind me of someone, I have this feeling of fate, and uh, your beauty is intimidating." "We must" she said, "get beyond beauty," and I had the distinct sense she was addressing some difficulty she carried in her portfolio. "You seem sincere enough," she said. "I can direct you back to the subway station so you won't get lost. This is a dangerous neighborhood for you." My heart sank. She was saying good-bye, and her remark about sincerity trivialized my turmoil. In my hopelessness I found my tongue. "I can only be honest with you, but the truth won't set me free." "Maybe," she said, "you expect too much from the truth." She extended her left arm for the return of her books. I brought the large text close to my face, it was Jansen's *History of Art*. The other was the Modern Library edition of Camus' *The Stranger*. "Poor Monsieur Meursault," I said. "Yes," she said, "the scrap of truth he hangs on to doesn't enrich his life."

And we were talking. First about the novel. We entered the projects. Bunches of young men and boys loitered on benches. A group of older men sat on chairs around a table playing dominoes and sipping cans of beer from brown paper bags. From somewhere came the sound of someone playing bongos, accompanying trumpets and a flute rendering a bolero. I guessed the trumpets and flute were coming from a portable radio, the accomplished percussionist on the bongos was somewhere in the more immediate dark.

She said, "I can't talk to you too long, my mother waits for me, and we're almost there." She said goodnight and waved to the round dark woman I could see through the glass of the door that opened into the lobby. The woman looked relieved, very glad to see her daughter. The mother looked at me, a swift and perfunctory assessment, and called to her daughter, "Elena avansa por favor." I said, "Elena? Can I see you again?" She said, "Try," and walked into the lobby.

All the tall buildings of the public housing project were identical; the cement walks wound around the towering buildings that made up a small city within the larger expanse of city. I couldn't find my way out. I might have asked the domino players, but I needed to calm down, quiet myself. It occurred to me that I should retrace my steps to the building Elena had entered so that I could get the number of the building and the name of the street.

It was all familiar. I'd been there only moments before, each time, each building, each door, identical. I persisted. The search was endlessly promising. I was happy. The sense of anticipation lasted all night.

Most of the windows in the towering monoliths were dark. The benches along the walk deserted. Some voices carried and faint music pulsed in the air. I heard an occasional police car or fire engine screaming. For a while I thought I'd find my way back to Elena's building, settle on a bench and wait for her to come out, in the morning. But I couldn't find the building, or if I found it I didn't know if it was the building, and too, I didn't want to give Elena the impression that I was stalking her; searching was okay, meeting by chance would be best, but I preferred to hedge my bet by finding the place where I'd be likely to see her.

I could see in the moon-bright sky the dim shapes of apartment houses that were not the public housing project, but despite my determined march, I couldn't get there.

The sound of the two walking behind me was sudden, some untended part of my reverie summoning me to attention. One was laughing. The other called, "Hey you." I kept walking, checked the sky that was getting light. First I thought the two guys might have been working the graveyard shift somewhere and just getting home. But the one laughing was too happy, maybe drunk. The two had been arguing, it sounded amiable. "You! Yeah you." I stopped, turned around. "That's right man. Don't ignore people when they call you." The laughing one said, "Take it easy Frankie." Frankie, carrying a large, flat package wrapped in brown paper crisscrossed with twine said something in Spanish, and "I'm cool." I stood facing them. They walked toward me. They were young, dressed in suits and ties and a little disheveled. "I wanna ax you a question," said Frankie. "Me?" "Yeah, you. I see you're not from around here. Don't be afraid we ain't gonna rob you." Frankie reached into his pocket, his hand swooped out, and the blade sprung. My joy held me. I might have been smiling, and from my adolescence I remembered boys laying three fingers on the blade of a pocket knife, measuring with an air of connoisseurship and saying, "Three inches to the heart" to indicate whether the knife was legal or a felony, the expert, knowing declarations suggesting that they could all be requisitely dangerous.

Frankie cut the twine and carefully unwrapped the brown paper from an ornate frame. The picture was about three feet long and two feet wide: on deep blue velvet a silver moon gleamed on a sumptuous gold surf lapping on a beach. The palm trees were gold. The stars were gems. There was a silver wriggle of a sailing ship's mast reflected on the curling waves ebbing on shore, "Whatta you think?" said Frankie. The question sounded like a challenge. His companion said, "I tole you it ain't real." Frankie said, "I ain't axin' you, I'm axin' him." I said, "It's a dream." "Yeah?" Frankie said, weighing my response, and then, "it's for the woman I love." "Well," I said, "she'll know you love her." "That's a good answer," said Frankie. I said, "Can you direct me to the nearest subway?" "You got to turn around, the other way, keep walkin' left 'til you're out of the projects and past Fort Apache," said Frankie. "Fort Apache?" "Yeah," the other said, "the police station, keep going, you can't miss the train station."

I stopped at a luncheonette and had two cups of coffee. There wasn't any point in going back to my apartment downtown. There wasn't time. I caught the express all the way to Canal Street and arrived at work a half hour early. At Dayton's Cafeteria I had another cup of coffee, a danish, and a cigarette.

I punched in at eight o'clock. We had to reorganize stock, moving goods from one loft to another. I loaded the cylinders of cotton and various synthetic cloths onto a hand truck, stacked it all into a freight elevator, and then unloaded and stacked it in bins in the upstairs loft. During the afternoon we loaded trucks for deliveries in the garment district and out of state.

I worked in a peculiar state of bliss. Toward the end of the day the tingling in my arms seemed to articulate a secret traveling in my blood to the tips of my fingers. I punched out at five-thirty, went to my locker, and discovered that I'd lost my textbooks. My notebook and the texts were probably on the floor of a subway car riding the circuit from lower Manhattan to Harlem. I hadn't written my name or address in the flyleaves; I hoped I could find inexpensive, used copies to replace the books I'd lost.

I headed for the subway. My class began at seven.

On the train, standing up, I was tired but not inclined to sleep. I thought I might remain awake until I saw Elena again. Standing, clutching a pole I craned my neck, wriggled to gain an inch, look around, humanity packed tight around me, someone's elbow in my stomach, the heavy scent of the cosmetics of a young woman with pitted skin overpowering, the tip of my nose less than an inch from hers: eyes opened face to face we managed to be blind to one another; my infinitesimal movements meant to allow me to search for Elena were misinterpreted by someone; a leg pressed my thigh. My flesh demurred, backing a sufficient millimeter away.

In class Professor Kleiner syllogized, dismantling whatever we presumed to know. I took notes on the envelope that held my electric bill. I scrawled, "Epistemological heebie jeebies"; but wrote nothing else as Professor Kleiner's lecture worked on me like a lullaby. White chalk dust on the swell of his buttoned vest, his insistent voice, benign, the yellowish lights overhead simulating daylight, the moon spattered miniscule white tongues on the night-filled windows. The snoring I heard was not my own and I reviewed my conversation with Elena. Engaged as I'd been by our discussion, a fabulous gift in itself, I was stunned from time to time and stared at her. She was cheerful and pulled me back to our discussion. From what she said and didn't say I gathered that she saw her beauty as some problem God had proposed and she was studying the phenomenon. Professor Kleiner placed a forefinger in his ear, removed it, examined the chalk dust on the tip of his finger as though reading from the white dust, and said, "Heraclitus reminds us that one can never step into the same river twice."

For most of the following week I was confident that I'd see her again. I spent several nights riding the subway to the Bronx, tried to retrace my steps, learned to find my way out of the housing project but never saw her. Midweek I walked all night to prove I could and no harm would come to me, and to provoke a good omen. Nuts with expectation, too much hope, at work nailing up a crate of goods I brought the hammer down on the thumb of my left hand. Zito the foreman gave me five bucks for a taxi and told me to go to the emergency room at St. Vincent's. The broken thumb was put in splints, bandaged, and throbbed all day.

By the end of the next week I began to mourn for what would never happen. I couldn't honor the grieving, nevertheless the power of it persisted, a pervasive fatigue that made every task difficult.

On Saturday night I sought a remedy. I willed myself out of my one-room apartment, walked down Avenue B and settled myself in a bar where most of the patrons, men and women, appeared to be celebrating something. The large gray-haired bartender with sympathetic eyes appeared oracular without having to say a word. I put down two boilermakers to lay a foundation and then stuck to beer. On a shelf behind the bar, above the rows of booze was a television showing a baseball game with the sound tuned so low no one at my end of the bar could hear it. Nevertheless everyone remained cordial. Several people fed the jukebox. The selection was eclectic. Dinah Washington sang "Love For Sale." Then I heard a polka and a chorus singing, "in Heaven there is no beer—that's why we drink it here." I decided on one more shot to reinforce my foundation before returning to beer.

A sublime soprano sang from *Madame Butterfly*, "Un Bel Di Vedremo." Someone in the bar cautioned, "Oh baby you're making a serious mistake." The bartender turned his head from the television and said something distinguishing between saints and martyrs I couldn't hear clearly, and then said, "Double play." I walked to the jukebox to find the name of the soprano. Some patrons were silent. Mostly those seated at the bar. Various groups at tables beyond the L-shaped bar were laughing, commenting as each monologist spoke to those present and projected his and her voice to be overheard by an unseen audience. I heard something very much like the nagging hope that propelled me through my nightlong walks. The clamoring contrapuntal choruses could be discerned one from another as I focused my attention on one at a time. At one table a group of three boys and two girls costumed like gypsies listened as one of the girls enumerated the horrors in the world—famine, war, environmental degradation, all perpetrated by their parents—and the children were indignant. A handsome middle-aged man with shoulder- length silver hair, red and blue paint on his face, stood at his table and reviled Picasso to two female acolytes young enough to be his daughters. The girls hung on his every word. He had a resonant baritone voice. The girls said something comforting. He broke off his denunciation of Picasso and recited "And Death Shall Have No Dominion." A patron at the bar walked to the jukebox and put a dime in for a reprise of "In Heaven There Is No Beer." The denouncer of Picasso concluded his recitation of Dylan Thomas, bowed to the applause at his table and began to dance what he called the Eros and Thanatos polka. The bartender called, "Greg, we don't have a license for dancing." The bartender's statement precipitated further dialogue on the freedom of expression, and at the far end of the bar there was applause for a home run. I wondered if the dancing painter hadn't exhausted his genius in creating an irresistible personality. One of the pretty acolytes asked, "Are you afraid of death?" He pirouetted and said, "Yes, that too."

On Sunday, modestly hung over, my bandaged thumb throbbing like radar, I became convinced that Elena was wandering through the Museum of Modern Art.

In the museum I searched for her and looked into the faces of the entranced as they stood before the Picasso etching, "Minotauromachy." The minotaur hovered over the horse rehearsing doom for Guernica: somnambulant on the horse's back lay a woman with melon breasts; a young girl held a votive candle above the mad horse's head, in the girl's other hand, a bouquet of flowers. On the extreme left, opposite the minotaur, Jacob with his head on backwards looked down from his ladder. Adjacent to Jacob on his ladder were two young women in nun-like repose, a pigeon on their windowsill, and tiny in the distance, a sailboat floated in nightmare gray. I couldn't find Elena.

Professor Kleiner clapped his hands in front of my face, the cloud of chalk dust made me sneeze; he said, "Young man, I wouldn't mind your coming here to sleep, but your snoring is making my lecture inaudible." The laughter around me was not unsympathetic. I said, "I'm sorry." Professor Kleiner said, "As I was saying, W.B. Yeats who believed in much nonsense, undoubtedly said it best, 'Man can embody truth but he cannot know it.'"

In the snack bar at Finley Hall lounge I drank a cup of bitter coffee and had a cigarette. I was almost certain that even if my eyes had closed while in class I hadn't entered into what could actually be qualified as sleep. I remembered that Elena's English had been too perfect, her pronunciation over precise, and her intonation supple only when she spoke Spanish. She had corrected my grammar. Maybe there was mercy, some prospect of moderation in my life in Elena's being an apparition. She laid her portfolio on the table and said "Hello." And I thought, she is present, talking to me because implicitly I've accepted as principle and precedent that one must give up all hope before our most ardent wishes are granted, and the requirement is frightening. But in a moment I was overjoyed.

We resumed talking as though there hadn't been any interval at all. She mentioned that she had to attend Math for Poets and the class was only offered in the evening, and she was fulfilling her physical education requirement with a fencing class that met in the late afternoon. I said that since I'd served in the army I wasn't required to take physical education, and I'd postponed Math for Poets because I was afraid I'd fail. She offered help.

We discussed Mersault's hopelessness, his desolation. I walked beside her, stood crushed against her in the subway car, red-faced, and followed her route above ground, through street after street, until she said, "We're not lost, but we have to retrace our steps," and laughed. I said, "Wait, tell me about the Pentecostals again."

The discussion of hopelessness had led us to consider

the intransigent longing for faith. Elena told me of her brief dalliance with the Pentecostals when she was fourteen. It was her mother who had led her there. She said that her mother remained Catholic and susceptible to every religious possibility. On the anniversary of the death of Elena's sister, Flora, lost in infancy, Señora Concepción's grief returned to the pain of the first moment. The year Elena turned fourteen, something in the tide of her mother's dreaming took her back to the first shock of grief. All Señora Concepción could communicate between weeping and hiccups was that going down on one's knees would be more efficacious than lighting candles. She took Elena by the hand to the storefront Pentecostal church. Elena said the tambourines and singing were beautiful. Señora Concepción shouted, "Hurry," and on the way to the Pentecostal church she managed to say that any possibility of grace requires surrender to God.

In the storefront church the powerful rhythm of the singing and tambourines mounted, and Elena thought, yes, I must surrender to God. But when she looked around and saw those surrendering to God, writhing, screaming, falling to the floor she was terrified and ran out of the church, away from surrender and her mother ran after her.

I told Elena about Reiko. Told her how I imagined that I was following Reiko. I reiterated my journey with Mr. Kim. Elena said that my hike with Mr. Kim had the character of a zen koan. I admitted that I remained puzzled.

Later I realized that Elena let me make love to her long before she allowed me to see her artwork. In my apartment, naked, on our knees in my bed, she showed me the painting and averted her face. Something akin to light stripping sensibility to the soul's mind, I was looking at the intricacy of an arrested instant of music, the scoring of something so rhapsodic that it could only survive as peace—or was it a schematic for a not yet extant harp, or a swooping sea gull's vision of sunlight sluicing through the cables of the Brooklyn Bridge. I made a belated come moan. She put her cheek next to mine and said that she loved my transparency and supposed my lack of guile made life difficult. A year later she said she loved me.

I remember the year as intervals between lovemaking, then talk, descents into the stories we told each other, Elena's stories epochs where I struggled like a ghost trying to be born into her history; and we ate many fine meals in moderately priced neighborhood restaurants.

There wasn't anything premeditated about the story each of us withheld; circumstances had to conspire to bring them to consciousness, the new thing in the life we shared making the telling possible; but we weren't spared shame for the nearly forgotten stories, even when memory had lapsed the tales shadowed the way we saw, and perhaps our capacity for loving.

In the first trimester of Elena's pregnancy her nausea was unrelenting and she had difficulty holding down food. Her obstetrician prescribed a medication to subdue the nausea. The medication ameliorated the sick feeling. For a while the queasiness eased during part of the day and Elena retained some portion of what she had eaten. But the medicine that worked to ease the nausea would also produce many of the symptoms of Parkinson's disease.

Elena's mother knew Elena was pregnant before Elena knew. Señora Concepción dreamt it and in the morning the sight of her daughter shuffling toward the coffee pot confirmed her dream. Señora Concepción attended early Mass and didn't inform Elena that she was "expecting" until that evening. Elena was surprised but accepted her mother's percipience, in these matters her mother had never been wrong. Women in the Project relied on Señora Concepción, her prognostications not only presaged conventional medical authority, she was far more accurate. Señora Concepción thought (and didn't hesitate to tell Elena) that her gift for book learning and her single-mindedness in creating inexplicable pictures had suggested a gift for celibacy, though only females who were very old, children, or cloistered away from the reach of male desire might be safe. Still Señora Concepción believed that something in Elena's character would enable her to remain chaste no matter how often she might be loved by a man. Motherhood, Señora Concepción recognized as another form of chastity.

Elena and her mother negotiated. I was allowed into the negotiations only after some primary issues had been settled. Señora Concepción had begun by saying her pacemaker had to be replaced and she spoke of the device as a homunculus enthroned in her heart, a tyrant who must be appeased. The creature placed in her heart by science reminded her several times a day of her mortality, and, Señora Concepción reminded Elena, giving special urgency to her arguments. Elena acceded to her mother's request that she be married in a consecrated house; but Elena would not agree to be married in the Catholic Church; she could not honor the inherent obligation to raise her child in the faith. Señora Concepción was confused by the fuss Elena made of this issue; here was her daughter marrying a Jew—which was no doubt a consequence of residing in the American Babylon, the city itself a confusion of blood and mind and out of the chaos came the material largesse of bread, shoes, and a television set, wonderful in themselves, nevertheless signs of the fall of the human race. Señora Concepción studied my face as I sat with the cup of coffee she had served me. I was one of the Creator's jokes she would take seriously. She said, "Yes, it is plain, this one too is crazy in love with you, but whether he has any of the reputed talents of his race to make your life easier remains to be seen. He is peculiar."

Finally Señora Concepción agreed to Elena's compromise; we'd be married in a Presbyterian Church; Señora Concepción considered the Presbyterians harmless, a church was a church, and the requirements of honor would meet at least this minimal standard. Señora Concepción urged that we marry quickly, before Elena began to show.

The unresolved and most embattled issue was Señora Concepción's insistence that we all live together, in her apartment. Señora Concepción repeated that now that Elena's brother José was away in the marines, his bedroom was available. And after all, Señora Concepción reminded Elena, it was Elena who had insisted on José's going away. Elena countered by saying she had only agreed with the judge's offer, which was really an ultimatum; either José serve in the Marines or serve time in Sing Sing. In the warfare with the Italian gang, two boys had been shot, one Italian, one Puerto Rican, and both would live the remainder of their lives as invalids. One Italian kid, honoring José's prowess with his fists testified that José hadn't availed himself of knife, gun, or lead pipe. It was this restraint that prompted the judge's leniency. And Elena, then and now, as she reminded her mother, felt that the odds of José's surviving in the Marines were significantly better then his chances in the neighborhood.

Señora Concepción reiterating the cruel truths the thing in her heart whispered, continued to make her case, as one who cannot help vocalizing the truths transmitted through her by a greater power. Elena should remember that her younger sister, Dolores was ten years old; in a couple of years Dolores would be a señorita (that is menstruous) and subject to new danger. And as Señora Concepción had to continue working in the factory, though she was always grateful for "la overtime," "el bosso" also insisted she bring home piecework and she had to rely on Elena to care for Dolores. Señora Concepción anticipated what Elena would say next. Yes, it was true that Tía Luisa was a great help, in fact indispensable. But devout and untouched Tía Luisa (Señora Concepción crossed herself) was getting on in years and, despite never having been married, her responsibility to her nephews and nieces (when asked, Tía Luisa calculated that she had seventeen children) kept her in constant transit throughout the five boroughs of New York.

Señora Concepción and Elena bargained and I conjured Tía Luisa as I'd seen her in a series of Elena's pen and ink drawings: a petite yet robust octogenarian, a wraith journeying sidewalks and subways, buoyant as a cork riding a stream in eternity where she'd insinuated herself when she was still a girl fraught with visions.

I made my offer to Señora Concepción to sweeten the deal. Elena hoped her mother would agree. I would give up my apartment on the Lower East Side and Elena and I would find a place within walking distance to the projects. The rents in the neighborhood were cheap and this was now a prime consideration. In the morning on the way to work I'd walk Dolores to St. Ann's school. Elena would wait for her at the end of the school day. Dolores would stay at our apartment until Señora Concepción could pick her up at the end of her workday. I'd arranged to take on as much overtime as possible at the warehouse and could meet household expenses and the cost of medical care for Elena and the baby. Living close by, Señora Concepción could see Elena as often as she liked; but Elena and I had to have a home of our own; moreover, I would find the time to accompany Señora Concepción to the doctor when she had to have her pacemaker attended to.

Señora Concepción noted that as a college boy I might be able to converse with the doctor, preventing him from slipping anything unwonted into her heart. She said I must be vigilant, smiled and added that her doctor was Jewish.

Señora Concepción with a great sigh agreed to the arrangement. We sat down to a meal of rice and squid and Elena's mother served me a glass of rum. I wanted a second glass but was able to refrain from asking for it.

We were married in a Presbyterian Church. Neighbors from the housing project attended the ceremony and the party at Señora Concepción's apartment. Señora Concepción had made Elena a beautiful white wedding dress. Walking in the street from the church back to the apartment, strangers stared at Elena and followed behind us all the way to the project. The strangers were welcomed to the party.

Neither of my parents attended the wedding. Although they were not religiously observant, my marrying a Gentile was seen as an act of betrayal, (unmitigated by their socialism) tantamount to conversion.

When I informed my father and mother (by telephone) that in the not too distant future they would be grandparents, my father, Elena, and I agreed to meet in a coffee house in Greenwich Village. My mother collapsed into bed and stayed there for two days. Her sister, my aunt Tessie, nursed her through shock to something that would have to serve as acceptance.

Within a week of meeting her, my father telephoned me with a scheme. "Such a girl should have a mink coat." He knew a guy who knew a guy. "Some mink coats fell off a truck." He offered to make arrangements for me to make installment payments, "and in a year, a year and a half you'll have the coat paid for." I explained that a mink coat wasn't a priority. Sounding brokenhearted he said, "Imagine her in a mink coat." When I said again that I wouldn't consider it, he said, "A liberal is a guy who can't put it all on the line," and slammed the phone in my ear.

I escorted Señora Concepción to the doctor and she took my arm when we crossed the street. She had helped us to find an apartment in a tenement five blocks from the projects. She bribed the superintendent with fifty dollars, the amount of a month's rent, added another twenty-five and got "El Super" to give the three rooms a fresh paint job. The walls were peach colored, the ceiling Caribbean blue. When I attempted to reimburse Señora Concepción, she refused the money. I slipped the money under the tablecloth on her kitchen table. Several days later Elena found under her pillow, three twenties, a ten, and a five dollar bill. Elena and I thanked her and accepted the money as a wedding gift.

Still Señora Concepción campaigned day after day to have us live with her. Elena bore the brunt of this; I was away working twelve-hour shifts, coming and going in the somber underground light and throbbing noise of the subway.

Sunday mornings we slept late. The pervasive racket of radios, televisions, domestic disturbances and traffic from the street moderated to a Sabbath hum. Señora Concepción visited in the afternoon bringing cod fish cakes, and rice and chicken. Dolores remained in the projects, playing with friends in a neighbor's apartment.

It was difficult to tell whether Elena's deep fatigue was because of the pregnancy, the incipient nausea, or the necessity of fending off her mother's incessant claims, but sometimes Elena cried. "Please," I said to Señora Concepción, and immediately she began to entertain; she could make us laugh. My mother-in-law was a brilliant storyteller; no matter how disparate the tales' themes, there was finally and always a hint of a concern central to Señora Concepción's life, some just claim she was entitled to make. Neither Elena nor I could resist her stories.

Elena nibbled at her food; I ate and listened ravenously. I dreamed Homer, round, female, and as monumental as Buddha. Señora Concepción said, "Do you remember the Irish priest at St. Theresa's, on Essex Street, recuerdas? He looked like a boiled egg. The one who had the affair with the Cuban Carmen? She and her sister Lydia worked with me in the factory on East Broadway. Lydia became the floor lady, remember? Lydia with the filthy mouth? She could even make Max the presser's face turn red. Always she bragged about the size of her husband's thing. When the other ladies begged, 'Please Lydia, such talk,' Lydia said, 'Why can't I tell, after all it belongs to me' and with her hands in the air as if measuring a giant squid her arms stretched wider and wider. They were a low family, but generous people. Lydia, you remember? She was the one who brought you perfume for your thirteenth birthday that I didn't allow you to wear. That was the year your father went out the door and didn't return. Anyway, Lydia's sister Carmen made that poor priest crazy. She wore rose tinted panties with "la cosa real" stitched in gold letters just below her navel."

Señora Concepción stopped speaking, shifted her bottom in the chair, squared her shoulders as if to bear the weight of all she knew, and said, "Ah, at least my nephew Ismael comes to visit me. Pobre muchacho." Elena said, "The muchacho must be fifty years old. "So," said Señora Concepción, "you remember him; after so many years he and his wife have moved back from Puerto Rico. They live in Brooklyn. Alleluia is dying. You remember Alleluia?"

Elena's head trembled, the cords in her neck rigid, her face taut with the effort to say something she didn't say, for a moment I saw a crone's skull through the face of a beautiful young woman. "Do you want to lay down for a while?" I asked. Elena's trembling head shook emphatically, "No."

Señora Concepción said, "I ask if you can remember because in no time at all people and their sacrifices are forgotten. Alleluia has cancer. The doctors cannot save her, though their treatment, Ismael told me, has made his wife bald. Do you remember how beautiful Alleluia was?" Elena said, 'Si.' "She looked like Sylvia Pinal of the cinema," said Señora Concepción, "and the poor girl afflicted with such beauty aroused the barbarous ecstasies of men, including her father and brothers—and unlike you she had no mother to protect her. Alleluia mourned her mother's passing and ran from her father and brothers, and Dios mio, the poor child had been running from the age of twelve while her mother was passing from this world to the next."

I watched Elena. Her head trembled and the muscles in her throat tensed. "Enough," I said, "Elena has to rest." Señora

Concepción agreed, brewed some special tea for Elena and went home.

When I suggested to Elena that we see the doctor and try to find out what was causing her trembling she said that could wait; she had a scheduled visit in two weeks. And as though she had made some Faustian deal, Elena said, she'd rather live with the trembling than the nausea.

Elena told me it was a Saturday when it happened. I was away, working overtime. She opened her eyes and my father was standing above her. I said, "Don't you lock the front door?" She said she had gone to the drugstore to renew her prescription and had probably forgotten to lock the door when she returned. Elena said, "I watched your father from the couch. First thing he did was to walk to the refrigerator in the kitchen and open the door to make certain it was well stocked with food. I was still half asleep. Your father called over his shoulder, 'Where's my son?' At first I'd forgotten that it was Saturday. I said, 'He's out, somewhere.' Your father said, 'Has he been asking you for clean underwear and handkerchiefs?' I said 'no.' He said, all right, that means he ain't playing around with a chippy, don't worry.' He came back to the living room with a large white box, opened it, and covered me with the mink coat. 'A wedding present from me,' he said. I drifted back to sleep under the warm coat."

Elena said, "I hope you're not angry." "About the coat?" "No, about the drawings I made, they are cartoon-like." I said, "No," and it was true; I was fascinated. Elena's drawing seemed to flesh out a dream I'd forgotten, given me access to something I might have once glimpsed. I turned the pages of her sketchpad. Saw the totemic rendering of my father's hawk-head, clearly, recognizably him, the bull's body zoot-suited as a nineteen forties hep cat, stalking something beyond sight, past Hymie's "Strictly Kosher Poultry Market" and the storefront "Iglesia de Dios Pentecostal."

On Sunday I awoke from a dream of a singing mustache. The dream might have been spawned by the reconciliation music of the couple whose window faced ours across the courtyard. They took turns beating one another up. When they reconciled they played a recording of a Mexican lament. On Sundays, before Señora Concepción visited, I usually played my favorite records and had a couple of drinks, which seemed to suffice. On that particular Sunday I didn't listen to my music or have anything to drink; I attempted another draft of "Chekhov Was A Doctor." I began with a description of my father with the hawk's head and bull's body. I was in love with what I'd written for several hours, then I saw that I'd failed. The chimera Papa I'd created was a fabulous monster, truly dangerous, but I'd failed to convey his lovableness, the kinship he fostered in spite of the havoc that always surrounded him.

My mother would never forgive him for the gift of the coat. Neither would she forgive me or Elena; we were all complicit in a ménage à trois betrayal. Mama repeated the story of the coat to her sisters for a decade. They recited it again and again to her, and when my father died, Elena didn't attend his funeral as the story of the coat and the payments my father made to a shylock for two years was certain to be wailed at her by my aunts, my mother's voice at the top of the chorus.

I'm not sure whether it was a Monday or Tuesday evening; I got home as usual at about eight-forty. Elena said she was feeling a little better. She'd had a nap, the nausea had abated for a while and she'd been able to cut down on the medication. She was barefoot, wearing a nightgown and the mink coat, devouring a wedge of avocado. She couldn't get enough avocado. Señora Concepción and I made certain that there was always an ample supply. Despite my end of the day stupor I had to touch her; she couldn't keep her hands off me. We tumbled on the couch. She raised her nightgown and didn't remove the coat. We burrowed into a rocking surcease, the feel of fur, and we came out of it after a time, laughing. Señora Concepción had come to the door and knocked; we never heard her. Later Elena showed me some bawdy drawings she'd made. I was a bicycle pump, pumping up a great pear shaped avocado that was her.

After the lovemaking I opened the convertible couch and we lay in bed. We talked for a while about when and how we might return to college. She said she wouldn't return to City College; she felt her portfolio was strong enough now to apply to Cooper Union and she asked me again if while I was at City I'd ever taken Professor Green's Introduction to Nineteenth Century Literature. I hadn't, but I'd heard a great deal about it from students who said it was great. Green, I'd heard, had moved on to a university in the Midwest. Elena said, "Yes, Iowa, or maybe it was Ohio." Again she told me he had been her first and only lover until she met me. This time she added details she hadn't told me before. My retrospective jealousy wasn't any greater than the first time I'd heard it; if anything I was calmer. Elena spoke as though she were surprised anew by the experience.

She said that Milton Green was handsome, charming, and his class enthralling. There was never any discussion during class. When the reading assignment was *The Brothers Karamazov*, Milton became in turn, each of the brothers, acting out the dialogue, and the class bore witness to Ivan's quarrel with God, Alyosha's holiness, Dmitri's innocent and murderous rage, Smerdyakov's corrupt rationalism, and the buffoonery of old man Karamazov's licentiousness. The class was always packed. All discussion took place after class in Findley Hall Lounge. Unlike most of the professors, Milton was accessible after his lecture and joined the students in discussion. "I knew," Elena said, "that he'd be my first lover." They met in an apartment in Greenwich Village. The apartment belonged to a friend of Milton's. Milton, Elena said, commuted from somewhere far out in Long Island.

She said he didn't wear a wedding ring, but she soon suspected he was married; he admitted that he was, and said he loved Elena. He also loved saying her name.

It lasted the semester. Elena said she didn't especially mind that he was married, only that he lied about it, seemed fearful much of the time, and after his urgent lovemaking was remorseful.

Elena said he described himself as a hostage to his desire. She found the role of femme fatale ludicrous but since it ignited his prurience she played the part and found a strange gratification in her ability to act. Sometimes he asked questions about her family like an anthropologist doing research.

Two weeks before the final (she hadn't told me this part before) Milton took Elena to a very posh restaurant and told her she wouldn't have to take the final exam; quite aside from "their relationship" he said, turning red and looking furtively at people at nearby tables, Elena's work in the course was outstanding. The waiter came to the table and displayed a bottle of wine and recited its pedigree. Elena said imperiously, "Professor Green, please hurry with the meal so you can take me back to the hotel and eat my pussy." Milton's hands shook, he dropped the wine glass.

Elena said that Milton's cowardice made her mean. Playacting, but nevertheless convincing, she had once chased him out of the apartment where they met with a butter knife. She said she laughed. He had left his jacket behind and was too frightened to return for it.

Professor Green completed the semester, but there was a rumor that he'd had a nervous breakdown. Elena signed the Get Well card that his students circulated and placed in his faculty mailbox. On the last day of classes, Professor Cummings, Elena's Sociology instructor, passed her a note asking if she might enjoy going bird watching with him. Elena declined the offer.

I didn't work the following Saturday. I awoke close to noon and Señora Concepción and Elena were setting the table for lunch. Dolores was walking on her hands. The child was a born acrobat, athletically gifted, almost always smiling except when she was at St. Ann's school. The nuns frightened her. Elena and her mother tried to comfort Dolores, and they agreed there wasn't an alternative; the public school was complete chaos and many children there were recruited as couriers for drug deliveries. When Dolores was liberated at the end of the school day she could hardly contain herself; she did cartwheels. She was still only when she sat in front of a television set. Señora Concepción couldn't understand how Elena and I could bear to live without one; and Dolores had complained that when she was at our home there wasn't any television.

Señora Concepción purchased, at the junkie's bazaar, a nineteen-inch television for us. She said she got it cheap, making her purchase as the market was closing down, the junkie's craving favoring her bargaining power, and she couldn't bear to see us living deprived. The television was installed in the living room. Dolores walked on her hands and settled herself before the screen. To get Dolores' attention once she was immersed in what was happening on the screen one had to shout and shake her shoulder.

Elena, Señora Concepción, and I were gathered around the kitchen table drinking coffee. I could no longer smoke in the apartment, the smell of smoke made Elena feel ill. I stepped into the hall for a quick smoke. When I returned Señora Concepción was saying she had gone to Brooklyn that week to visit Alleluia at the hospital. She said that the doctors had made it clear that Alleluia couldn't last much longer. The morphine drip had mercifully muted her pain. People appeared at her bedside asking for forgiveness, and reassuring her that she'd recover: two cousins, an aunt, a brother and Ismael, whom she recognized, but these people coming in succession, appearing out of a haze, making her the center of attention, wanting something, were only delaying the fulfillment of her desire to finally get away.

Señora Concepción said she wouldn't be able to visit Alleluia again. It wasn't that Alleluia could only identify Señora Concepción as an acquaintance she couldn't quite place, but the lights in the hospital, Señora Concepción said, and all the machines Alleluia was connected to "spoke to the thing that sits on my heart and told it to beat faster, like I was a girl dancing, and I'm not a girl anymore. My blood flowed backward and I got dizzy."

"You should," Señora Concepción said to Elena, "take the opportunity to say goodbye to her; she was once your friend." An old woman's palsy rattled Elena's head. She said, "I can't." I thought her lips looked a bit swollen. Señora Concepción nodded to indicate she understood. From the living room came the inane melody of a Tom & Jerry cartoon. A cat and mouse chase exploding into the crashing of pots and pans.

Señora Concepción paused and went on. I wanted to hear more. Elena remained at the table, compelled to listen for reasons I misunderstood.

Lydia and Carmen, Señora Concepción said, were the first to come to Alleluia's aid. They could see she was lost and frightened. She sat on the stone stoop of their building, a cardboard suitcase open on the step beneath her. She searched in the suitcase, which contained one blue cotton dress, a pair of slippers, and a banana peel. Lydia said that what Alleluia hoped to find was either lost or had never been there. When finally Lydia and Carmen coaxed Alleluia to speak, they learned that she had been searching for the home of a cousin she couldn't locate. An arrangement had been made for Alleluia to live there. It seemed that the cousin had moved. Alleluia counted her money. She had two dollars and forty-seven cents. When she ventured beyond the surrounding streets she couldn't find anyone who spoke Spanish. Carmen asked her how old she was. Alleluia said fifteen. Lydia and Carmen thought she looked younger.

Alleluia did find in the pocket of her blouse a crumpled piece of paper with the name of a Maria Perez scrawled on it and one eleven or eleven, the writing was smudged, Ludlow Avenue. Lydia said she knew of Ludlow Street, which was nearby, but she'd never heard of Ludlow Avenue. Regarding Maria Perez, Carmen said the phone book would probably list many, and she and Lydia would help Alleluia search for her cousin.

They couldn't find the right Maria Perez and Lydia and Carmen took Alleluia in to live with them. After a couple of weeks Lydia and Carmen arranged for Alleluia to try out at the factory, where she met Señora Concepción. It was true, as Alleluia claimed, she could sew. But she was much too slow, given to weeping, and too many flights to the bathroom. Carmen and Lydia had hoped that the job would allow Alleluia to be self-supporting and find her own apartment. As Señora

Concepción had predicted Alleluia did eventually become adept at the sewing machine, but back then, she barely lasted the week at the factory.

Lydia and Carmen would not put Alleluia out in the street. At the factory they complained, said Alleluia was a burden and they couldn't support her forever. After a month Señora Concepción took her in.

At the factory Lydia and Carmen told Señora Concepción everything. They said when their cousin Roberto came to visit, at once, upon meeting Alleluia, he said, "Enchanted," and began to do everything to her with his eyes. Lydia said she felt culpable for what had happened; Cousin Roberto had been born in the States, still he had no visible means of a livelihood, sometimes needed a place to sleep, and she and Lydia had given him a key to the apartment. Roberto, they said, was a marvelous dancer, much in demand as a partner at the Palladium where he searched for a possible young widow, or beauties beginning to age who were invariably sympathetic to him. He was also a compulsive gambler and his movement around the city was constant. He was always in trouble, but Lydia and Carmen said his charm never deserted him. Carmen maintained that Alleluia must have led him on, encouraged him in some way. Lydia asserted that she loved her cousin but couldn't believe that Alleluia was at fault.

It wasn't clear to Alleluia whether Roberto or her brother Paco was the father. When finally Alleluia confided to Señora Concepción, neither did she clarify whether Roberto had seduced or raped her. Roberto, in his ardor, couldn't make such a distinction and Alleluia under the pall of morning sickness, and the shame of the world about to fall on her, wasn't inclined to differentiate the vagaries of love as she begged Señora Concepción for help.

Señora Concepción, from an act of simple kindness felt herself drawn into deeper and more complicated trouble. She offered to take the child Alleluia didn't want to bear. Desperate, Alleluia lacked discretion and begged for help all over the neighborhood. She vowed that she would scrape the face of her violator out of her womb. Someone, Señora Concepción learned, had recommended Doña Gracia. Although Doña Gracia was neither especially venal nor a person of ill will, neither was she especially competent. And Alleluia was determined to have an abortion.

Ismael, Señora Concepción said, was at least twenty years older than Alleluia. He worked for the post office, hadn't married, and bought a house in a desirable neighborhood where he lived with his widowed mother. Everyone knew, Señora Concepción said, that her nephew Ismael was a serious and industrious man. When Ismael came to visit, he was immediately taken by the beauty and fair skin of Alleluia. Her thick golden hair gave him a fever. His need to shed his bachelorhood emerged suddenly. In spite of what Alleluia confessed and Señora Concepción confided, he proposed marriage within days. Ismael, the hard-working brown man, dreamed of fair skinned children, children who could rise in the world, as this is the privilege of fair skin. Ismael promised Alleluia lifelong devotion and spoke in his most gentle and serious voice. He explained he couldn't live with the prospect of a black child, especially a child with the face of the black Cuban Roberto, Alleluia's violator, eating at his table, living under his roof; ridding her womb of the past was a practical necessity, Ismael reminded Alleluia. She could, he said, leave misfortune behind.

Neither Señora Concepción's remonstrations nor any story she could tell could dissuade Alleluia. She had even told her the story of her mother Beatriz: not because she expected it to persuade Alleluia, but Señora Concepción believed the story her mother had told her exemplified that hope like desire was sometimes satisfied. Her mother Beatriz, Señora Concepción said, had already given birth to twelve children. Beatriz, Señora Concepción reckoned, was not old, but she looked old, stringy, muscular, and harried. Her husband Hector was a hard working and strangely imperturbable farmer. In addition to the usual manly labors he was skilled at sewing and made all the children's clothing. Beatriz, a dutiful wife never denied her husband, but she could no longer bear to look at his smiling face. When Beatriz missed her monthly she became desperate at the thought of a thirteenth child. She fell to her knees and prayed to the Virgin for help. She prayed incessantly and with all her heart. When Beatriz fell asleep at night in complete exhaustion she snored with her mouth wide open, the inhalation and exhalation of her breath sounded like a train roaring through a tunnel. Usually Hector slept through Beatriz's snoring. But on the night of the storm the sounds coming from Beatriz's gaping mouth were drowned out by thunder and lightning. He awoke. The earth shuddered. Tree limbs and birds were blown about, the ocean stood up, the shutters and doors were blown from the house, and Beatriz with her mouth wide open went on sleeping. Hector saw it. The lightning flashed from the toiling green sky through the window into Beatriz's open mouth.

In the tranquil morning Hector and Beatriz concerned themselves with replacing the roof of their house. Beatriz knew that the Virgin had intervened. The lightning from heaven had entered her mouth and scooped the child from her womb and given it to a rich but kind and barren woman who had longed for a child all her life. Beatriz knew Doña Consuelo and brought her a basket of fruit once the news of Doña Consuelo's pregnancy was general gossip in the village. Beatriz's monthly arrived several days late, her bleeding was more ample than usual, but she didn't feel indisposed.

Alleluia said she was willing to sleep with her mouth open and hope for a storm, but she reminded Señora Concepción that Beatriz's deliverance only happened after she'd had twelve children.

Finally Señora Concepción gave in and asked Alleluia to at least seek the services of Dona Angelica who was reputed to be more skilful than Dona Gracia. Señora Concepción offered money to help. Alleluia said Ismael had already provided a sufficient sum.

Meanwhile, Roberto, incapable of believing that Alleluia could surrender to anyone but himself, suffered remorse and tender feelings. The experience was new and confusing. The disruption of his repose a shock. Between his dancing life and the circumlocutions of his perpetual fugitivehood Roberto had found a rhythm that engendered poise. But now he missed a step, stumbled when he danced, couldn't read his cards, play the hand that was dealt to him; the dice endlessly rolled snake eyes. He found that he'd drifted into clubs he knew he should avoid. He wondered whether someone had put voodoo on him; was there some ill will, some retribution stalking him that he must appease. He concluded that he had to do something that would prevent his good luck from being banished forever.

Although an offer of marriage never occurred to Roberto, he was surprised to remember that Alleluia had spoken of a fountain in the plaza of her hometown. She hadn't really spoken to him, but wept and spoke to herself, transported back in time, when she was safe and happy. She was a child and her mother had taken her to the plaza where Alleluia played at the fountain. Roberto attempted to speak to Alleluia. She, deep in recollection spoke to herself, at last calm, wistful. She said that certainly the fountain could not have been as grand as she remembered. But it was beautiful and she was always at peace there. The fountain, she conjectured, wiping her eyes and smiling, as though she might have been speaking to her long gone mother, the fountain may have been some three feet tall; it was made of wrought iron, fashioned into a daisy with birds made of braided wire perched on each petal; water sprouted from the heart of the daisy and the base of the fountain was concrete. Alleluia had set orange peels sailing in the fountain and studied their cruising in the widening ripples of water.

Roberto took the midnight flight to Puerto Rico. The midnight departure time, dubbed the "cha-cha" flight, required a fare of only sixty dollars; this too contributed to the inevitability of the enterprise. Lydia said that Roberto had helped himself to the money she and Carmen had set aside and placed beneath their underclothing in a drawer of the bedroom dresser. This had happened before, and on a number of occasions Roberto had eventually returned money to them.

Lydia and Carmen were not surprised that their cousin had stolen the fountain from the town square. How he had planned, if he had a plan, to transport his gift to Alleluia in the Bronx was a mystery.

By the time Señora Concepción learned the story there were several versions. Each based on several indisputable facts. It was not difficult to believe that Roberto was brazen enough to be hammering away in the predawn hour at the cement and tile moorings of the fountain. Whether Roberto had stolen or purchased the tools that enabled him to carry off the fountain was a detail that neither Señora Concepción nor Lydia nor Carmen felt compelled to determine. But they did argue about the townspeople. Señora Concepción didn't believe that so many residents had slept soundly, and those who hadn't, had been cowed by a criminal reckless enough to be hammering away in the predawn light. Carmen and Lydia wanted to believe that their cousin had intimidated the town. Señora Concepción believed that this was filial loyalty and Cuban patriotism, which more often than not was a conceit that she, as a Puerto Rican, could detect in her nostrils.

What is certain is that Roberto was found floating face down in the surf, as though studying the coral ocean floor, his guts open to the sea life swimming in and out, the fountain toppled in the shallow, splashing tide. The tide rolled him over, and his open eyes appeared to be searching the clouds for a way to transport the fountain to Alleluia in the Bronx, a difficult but not impossible task. He floated on his back and his posture suggested that his last thought conceded that his redemptive act was incomplete, but he was satisfied with his effort.

Señora Concepción asserted that Roberto had been slaughtered by civic outrage, and the fact that Paco and another of Alleluia's brothers had been present was only incidental; the notion that they were exacting revenge for the dishonor of their sister was an embellishment added to the story later.

Elena and I were in bed when she picked up where her mother left off. The swelling of her lips had increased, the cords in her neck were tense and her head trembled. She still resembled herself, the shuddering head prescient of an old woman battling the betrayal of her body. I said to Elena that we must see the doctor. She said her scheduled appointment was only a week away and that since she had begun the medication the nausea had become infrequent and tolerable.

Alleluia, said Elena, was convalescing. "Never," Elena's mother would say, "would I have put Alleluia in your bed if I knew." There had been a reorganization of sleeping arrangements. Elena's bed was moved to her mother's bedroom, and her mother's bed was moved to what had been Elena's bedroom so that when Dolores awoke in the middle of the night she still stumbled to the same bedroom and the same bed, but now she cushioned herself against her mother's soft body, and this proved satisfactory. José, when he was not prowling the streets, slept on the couch that opened into a bed in the living room. Narcisso, Elena's father was rarely home, most of the time he was off in the throes of courtship of his most recent inamorata. Señora Concepción saddened, but long ago having accepted the inevitable said, "Because of your father there are so many horns growing out of my head that I'm unable to comb my hair."

Lying in the warm tide of bedclothes, twelve year old Elena clasped Alleluia, the two exchanging breath, Elena dreamed of her body taking on womanly shape from the fifteen-year-old Alleluia's luminous flesh; Alleluia's beauty beset by all it inspired, just like Sylvia Pinal in the movies.

Alleluia's drama traveled from the dark of Elena's dreaming to the dark of the cinema, where Elena bore witness in the drifting clouds of cigarette smoke, Señora Concepción seated beside her, nodding to the truth enfolding on the screen. Sylvia Pinal, Señora Concepción, and Elena's favorite actress was the lovely and innocent country girl walking on the road toward the main house of the estate where she would work as a servant. The patron, Don Francisco, cantered by on his black stallion. The patron, overwhelmed by the girls' beauty, dismounted and took the girl by force. Don Francisco, habituated by his seigniorage to what he assumed his privilege, afterward experienced the beginning of a doubt. What Elena and Señora Concepción saw on the screen as the moment of violation was the patron's boot, grinding the rose he plucked from the girl's hair into the muddy road. For a year the patron, alternately mad with lust or remorse, kept the girl hostage. The girl escaped to a nunnery where she gave birth to a son she surrendered to an orphanage, and she remained at the place where she found refuge and became a nun.

The son grew to be a man and a fine physician. He embarked on his early adventures, the most salient being his rescue of a girl from the fate of his mother, in nearly the same circumstances of his mother. Though the young man had no way of knowing this: the young doctor, with the help of a beggar soothsayer who found him worthy, at last found his mother. She was an aging nun afflicted with cataracts; still she made her way through the dark canonical hours and knew her son's voice as soon as she heard it. The doctor operated on his mother's cataracts and her eyes cleared long enough to see her son's face before she hastened from this world to her reward. Elena and Señora Concepción saw Sylvia Pinal's lovely face, which was Alleluia's face, hidden in a nun's wimple, serene and forever young.

The final tableau of the movie moved slowly to celestial music to reveal how all were transformed: the doctor son devoted his life to serving the poor, Don Francisco dedicated himself to charitable works and contemplation, transfigured through remorse to moral splendor, the prime mover the angelic beauty of Sylvia Pinal—Alleluia.

In bed, Elena's belly pressed against mine, our child kicked, the blow reverberating from Elena's womb south, below my navel; Elena said, "Oh," the hair on my groin prickled, and Elena and I entangled our ankles.

Elena said she wasn't sure that Alleluia admired her drawings. Alleluia was exhausted and tolerant. Tucked in bed, beneath a clean sheet and blankets, their heads propped on a pile of pillows, twelve-year-old Elena was making an offering, seeking some sort of recognition from Alleluia. Alleluia's head sunk deeper into the pillow. Elena held her drawing in front of Alleluia's face. The drawing depicted the moment when the chaste Sylvia Pinal, the innocent girl of the country, is violated by the patron. Elena's composition focused on what the movie audience had been allowed to see, the brutal heel of the patron's boot grinding the rose he'd plucked from the girl's hair into the muddy road. Elena's face veiled by her drawing, she heard Alleluia breathing. She peeked; Alleluia's eyes had closed. Elena appreciated that Alleluia, embattled by love, was tired and distracted; still each night, in sleep, they clung to one another. In Elena's dream the ocean was cleansing but the image of the rose ground into the muddy road festered and propelled her from sleep.

Elena heard the sirens of fire engines. People screaming roused her from the wet tangle of bedclothes. Perhaps the siren was an ambulance, or a police car. She thrashed free of the warm sheets tugging at her ankles. Awake she knew the red was blood. Her nightgown and the bed were wet. Alleluia lay there, wide-eyed, silent, bleeding.

Señora Concepción ran to the bedroom, screamed, genuflected, and sprinkled Holy Water on Alleluia and the blood soaked bed. It was Saturday night. Elena heard music. One siren screamed close by, another in the distance. Something was lodged in her throat. She could smell smoke. Torching abandoned buildings had become popular among the young, amateur arsonists. Her mother was shouting at her. Elena looked at the blood dripping from the hem of her nightgown. She nodded and ran for help.

When Doctor Ziesel arrived Alleluia was curled into a fetal position clutching a crucifix. Neighbor women surrounded the bed praying, cursing men, and beseeching the Virgin Mary for help. Elena thought that Doctor Ziesel (perhaps the last physician in New York to make house calls) resembled a benign Groucho Marx. Life had scoured from his face the possibility of anything sardonic. The doctor's bald dome glistened pink and feverish, above his ears hair as dense as steel wool jutted into corkscrews; he appeared at the point of weeping that never happened because of haste, and coping with perpetual emergency. Doctor Ziesel, like Alleluia, had been in flight since childhood from pursuing armies. He lurched inside his large, baggy pinstriped suit, carrying the little black bag with medical instruments, his pockets bulged with medicine. He arrived as always, harried and alert. He whispered to Señora Concepción because informers were everywhere.

He saved Alleluia's life and fled. Señora Concepción considered that Doctor Ziesel, his comic shamble, and grief fixed on his face like a clown's painted mask, might be a saint. Doctor Ziesel had also been willing to examine Tía Luisa without requiring her to disrobe. Señora Concepción prayed for the safety of Doctor Ziesel. She suspected that her prayers had been answered. Doctor Ziesel had been mugged twice, injured seriously once, and still he continued making house calls along the way to the messianic border, beyond which was safety.

When Elena awoke she realized that she hadn't been embracing Alleluia, the weight in her arms was made of longing and a pillow, and she remembered that Doctor Ziesel and her mother had arranged for Alleluia to continue her convalescence with a relative of Ismael's in Brooklyn. Elena was in bed alone, the scent and heat of Alleluia still all about her. Elena searched the dark. She'd made the bed with the new white sheets her mother had given her. When she saw the spots of blood she called for Alleluia in a hushed voice. The adamant silence didn't answer, the beginning of light washed through the window, and over the bed sheets she saw more blood. She closed her eyes, clenched her teeth, and crossed her arms over her breasts. She remembered that her friend Isabel, the first girl in their class to have breasts, had spoken of the "curse."

Her mother explained that the blood was her own and it signified the beginning of her woman's life; moreover, Señora Concepción instructed, on those rare occasions when her father visited she could no longer sit on his lap.

In bed Elena told me the rest. I said that I was going out to find a cab, and we'd go to the hospital. She said, "You'll stay and listen." When I started to get out of bed she screamed, "pay attention!" and slapped my face. The heat across my cheek subsided and I tasted blood in my mouth. Her head and hands were trembling, her neck rigid. I reached for the fur coat folded over the back of the chair next to the bed, and draped it around her shoulders. The shaky voice said, "I'm not cold." She let me hold her hand. Her lips were swollen and her tongue pressed against her front teeth as though trying to hold them in place. "Narcisso," she said, "my father," squeezing my hand. I saw an old woman. She said that her mother had told her that Narcisso was a man too much in love with his freedom to love anything else. He himself was not brutal although the consequences of his leave taking were. In the year that Alleluia married Ismael, and Elena had become a señorita, Narcisso appeared on Father's day with flowers he presented to Señora Concepción. This happened annually, though sometimes it was on Easter or during the Christmas season. Jose threatened to throw him out of the apartment. Señora Concepción rebuked José and he stormed out and took himself to the gym, where he stayed for days, sleeping on a cot in the locker room. Jose had been recruited for the Golden Gloves and he was looked upon by the Catholic Youth Organization coach as a very promising prospect. Coach Duggan insisted that if Jose was serious about realizing his talent, he focus his attention on boxing to the exclusion of every distraction.

Señora Concepción berated Narcisso, screaming in his face, gripping the flowers he'd given her; she gave a detailed account of his betrayals, moral weakness, his every lack as a real man. He smiled and agreed with everything she said. Crying and in a rage, Señora Concepción raised her hand to smack the fecklessness from his face. Narcisso's face grew rosy from the blows. Then, as always, he reminded her that they had been married in a church and never divorced: whatever the dalliances that kept him busy he had given his name to their children, which was something he'd never done for any of his infatuations. Implicit in this, as Elena knew, was his claim of conjugal rights. And Elena also knew her mother was powerless to resist.

Finally I coaxed Elena to the door. She was wearing the mink coat, a bathrobe underneath, and I removed her slippers and put her shoes on. We could probably find a cab on Third Avenue. She was still narrating, urgently; her lips were bulbous looking, her tongue was swelling out of her mouth and I wiped a string of saliva from her chin.

Her mother had to have been sleeping. When Dolores had fallen asleep Señora Concepción had carried her to the convertible couch in the living room. Elena, exhausted by the agitation and confusion her father's rare visits provoked, slept deeply. It was like a dream. A touch light as a butterfly. A hand that might have been her own tracing the swelling of her emerging breasts. When she opened her eyes, Narcisso standing above her apologized at once. He took his hand away, kneeled by the bed, and confessed. He said that the cause of his deserting the family was Elena; if he had remained he would have been powerless to resist.

In the cab on the way to the hospital Elena and I agreed. It was absurd for her to feel responsible: to accept that she had to bear the burden of the desire she provoked, as men are not capable of such restraint, being inherently bestial—and therefore women must sustain morality in the world—she said she would always resist this hypocrisy. Her head trembled, each palsied word fell out wet, her swelling tongue licked her enlarged lips; click-clacking guttural sounds enveloped every word. I discovered the acoustics of her speech, and the cab driver glancing over his shoulder looked frightened and drove faster.

The emergency room was crowded. The Saturday night casualties jammed the room. Gurneys and wheelchairs were loaded with the sick and injured. Every metal folding chair was occupied. Some of the hurt and ill stood leaning against the wall. One mother sat rocking a wailing infant, another clamped between her knees a little boy racked by coughing. A man with a broken arm paced the floor and howled. A tall, middle-aged nurse with a neutral face distributed forms and pencils.

Elena, oddly comforted, beauty annulled, her swelling tongue protruding from tuberous lips, experienced the novelty of anonymity; almost always, in any crowd one or more males would find a pretext to attend to her. Now there was a kind of privacy; she could spy on the world, and have her thoughts without having to invent a response to attention she didn't desire. I shouted that she was innocent, almost drowned out by the howling, weeping, the tantrums of the walking wounded, the ringing of bells and the urgent calls of charging orderlies pushing gurneys loaded with those closest to death.

I didn't know if Elena could find absolution, and I didn't

know what else to say to convince her, but I couldn't quit. She, with her tongue hanging on her chin like a thrashing pinfish, her deep-sea language of clicks, clacks and gurgling arpeggios agreed with me but remained unconvinced. Of course, we agreed it was beyond reason. Once again I said that it was crazy for her to harbor responsibility for her father's deserting the family because he feared he couldn't resist his incestuous desire for his daughter. His confession to her was itself some sort of lunatic malice. Elena indicated with her eyes, which were swifter than her bloated tongue, that this was not news to her. She was innocent and couldn't believe in her innocence; she was guilty and couldn't believe in her guilt, and she couldn't atone for whatever it was she was a party to.

Next to us, sprawled in a wheel chair, an unconscious man bled heavily from a wound on the top of his head. His chest was heaving. I called to the nurse who'd been distributing forms and pencils and was now crouched down talking to the little boy with whooping cough. I called to the nurse and pointed to the man in the wheelchair. I thought he might be dying. The nurse shouted back, "Oh, that's Eddie. He's here every Saturday night." The nurse pointed to the dispensary, directing the mother and the little boy, "Medicine," she said, "the pharmacy, yes, that way." The nurse circumlocuted around a tottering drunk, squeezed by a gurney where a man had raised himself on one elbow, protested, and clawed the air reaching for her. She moved the wheelchair with Eddie in it, comatose and bleeding; she looked at Elena, turned, and asked me to explain. I told the nurse about the medicine to combat the nausea, and said, "Yes," Elena was probably at the end of her third month. Elena repeated that certainly she must be at the end of the third month. The nurse couldn't understand a word Elena said. Elena nodded yes. I repeated, "Right, the end of the third month." The nurse said that some women had a reaction to the medication Elena had been taking, the medicine did sometimes cause the symptoms of Parkinson's disease. Elena, she said, should stop taking the medicine and the symptoms would quickly disappear. In the meantime she'd give Elena an injection that would hasten that process. Elena asked what she could do if the nausea returned. The nurse asked, "What did she say?" I told her. The nurse said that as Elena was completing her trimester the nausea would probably subside. She said she'd return to give Elena the injection and then we could go home. The nurse turned and barreled through swinging green doors where a large policeman now stood as a sentinel. I had more questions and wanted to talk to a doctor.

About an hour before daylight a doctor appeared. Elena's head rested on my shoulder, she was sleeping. The doctor repeated what the nurse had said hours ago, (she'd never returned) gave Elena an injection in the upper part of her arm, and we left the emergency room. The crowd had thinned out. Eddie was still there, crapped out in the wheelchair, but his head had been cleaned up and bandaged.

We didn't have enough money for a cab home and traveled by subway. It was Sunday morning; the trains were slow in coming. Waiting and riding it took about an hour and a half to get home. We drowsed on the train. When we awoke, got out of the train, and walked the quiet Sunday morning streets I saw that what the doctor had said was true. I was looking at the beautiful Elena again, the trembling and the disfigurement were gone. Back home, in the kitchen, I asked Elena if she wanted an avocado, she said, "No, steak."

I was offered additional overtime at work and accepted; the money was good. Part of the business at American Mills was a textile remnants operation. The pieces of cloth cut from patterns on the cutting tables at garment factories were collected in bins beneath the cutting tables and salvaged by me and my coworkers, when the cutters took a coffee break. We stuffed the rags and remnants into burlap sacks and trucked the stuff to a loft in the warehouse, where we sorted the goods according to quality, then baled it up and shipped the bales to mills in New England that specialized in reprocessed wool. The work was dirty and heavy. We maneuvered the bales, which averaged five hundred to eight hundred pounds with baling hooks and hand trucks. The air in the loft was so thick with textile dust that at the end of the day I spit rainbows. I was getting home at about ten each night. Our pay came in envelopes, cash, and a slip explaining the accounting of hours; straight time, time and a half, and double time for Sunday. Elena started a savings account.

I climbed out of the subway, stiff, numb across the shoulders; my fingertips and palms calloused from the constant handling of burlap sacks and the bales wrapped in burlap, no longer felt the texture of skin, though the flesh beneath was alive to pressure, as though I were always wearing thick gloves.

Elena said my hands rasped her skin but she didn't back away from my touch. I navigated from the bed to the street, to work and home again in a delirium; happy, mad, trudging agape through my blessed life. Elena no longer felt ill. Wearing a coat she didn't appear pregnant. Out in the street, shopping, she felt herself recapitulating her former life; relearning the strategies that allowed her to move on with her daily business as the grocer served her with elaborate courtesy, and prolonged the transaction as long as possible, the fruit vendor insisted on making a gift of the cantaloupes, and the butcher had taken to wearing cologne, much to the amusement of his wife, who watched him closely and shouted at him to pay attention to his work, as he had barely missed hacking off his left hand while preparing pork chops for Elena.

On a Friday night, after working twenty-one consecutive twelve-hour days, I found myself looking forward to the weekend. I carried my week's pay in my pocket. Three blocks from home a sweet-faced kid who looked too young to be out after dark asked if I could spare some change. I spit quarter-sized rainbows on the pavement and fished in my pocket. He heard the coins jingling and his eyes lit up. The lanky guy who stepped out of a doorway was about a head taller than me. He wore a raincoat that came down to his ankles, white sneakers, and a beret. His eyes were dead and his voice reassuring, "Just be cool." He said, "Please, don't make me do something I can't confess to my priest." His blade hovered near my eye. The little kid, as though he'd been remiss said, " Oh, this is my cousin Raymond," looked worshipfully at his cousin and brandished from behind his back a car aerial. Someone came up behind me. Raymond said, "That's Paulie, he's helping out."

They left me subway fare for the morning. The adrenalin cooking in me precluded sleep. My negligence haunted me; I couldn't afford a gun and bought a switchblade. On my toes, adrenalin simmering, I moved through the land of Nod. Every two or three days I fell into bed and knew the frightening dreams were dreams, and I could end my helplessness by simply opening my eyes.

In the hallway it was always night. The odor of fried food seemed to thicken the dark. Murmurings of music, dissonant, blending, strident and soft flowed into a cavernous echo, a requiescant hum at the bottom of the sea. The laughter of the kids under the stairwell bellied up, hysterical, breaching the solemnity of a wake, about to become a riot. They smoked reefer when they had it and sniffed glue. The remnants of what had been a large Irish community, they made valiant forays out into the street battling the Puerto Rican and Black gangs, outnumbered and outgeneraled. The boys affected the esprit de corps of the doomed. They repaired to the void under the stairwell for rest and recuperation. Elena and I lived three flights up. When I reached the dimly lit steps for the climb home I was joyous, exhausted and crazy; and I could see in the dark. Or maybe I perceived through some reborn, animal faculty. One lambent shadow moved out from under the stairwell; for him the dark wasn't dark enough, and he wore sunglasses. His elegant and enervated junkie's glide carried him past me and I couldn't tell whether he was nodding to me in neighborly greeting or nodding out.

On Saturday morning Elena and I took the subway downtown to Fourteenth Street. There was an art supply store near Cooper Union where she got her stuff at a discount. She was excited and looking forward to working with color again. We also had to shop for groceries. We got home at about one. It was a bright, clear day. My arms were loaded with grocery bags. Elena carried a cloth shopping bag with her paints, brushes, a pint of turpentine, and a jar of linseed oil; she had an ample supply of canvas at home. We stepped from the brightness of the street to the submarine darkness of the hallway. There was either the beginning of a fight or a party under the stairwell. The dark shapes of bodies flew out from under the stairwell and ricocheted off the wall, laughing and cursing. I blocked one by turning my shoulder, shifting the bags in my arms; he was about to collide with Elena. He bounced off me and sprawled on the floor. There was a lake of white across the front of his windbreaker, white speckled the murk of his face. He bellowed "Motherfucker." Those around him convulsed with laughter. The container of milk in one of the bags I carried had been crushed in our collision. My jacket was damp. Elena and I stepped around the body, squeezed by the others and started up the stairs.

We were halfway up the first flight of stairs when I heard "Oh Mama, I wanna taste a you." I smelled the words before they were said, spun around, the groceries still in my arms, and peered down into a face I could hear leering. Whatever it was I yelled made him look bad in front of his friends, and they laughed and goaded him. “You gonna let him get away with that? He talking to you like you a punk! Woa, there is some shit you don’t eat, Danny boy.” The vernacular of these Irish kids was almost identical to that of the Black and Hispanic kids. Elena and I continued up the stairs. When we reached the next flight I heard the footsteps plodding up behind us; the voices behind the footsteps, goading, egging him on, “You gotta do what you gotta do. Jive asses ain’t allowed to hang out here.” Elena above me, said calmly, “Let’s just go home, my ankles hurt.” I felt my face burning, the hair on the back of my neck alive, a prickling rushed over my skin. I was anxious to have Elena off the steps, away from this. She said, “Please,” more in exasperation than anything else. We continued climbing the stairs. I could hear the footsteps following behind us, the voices pushing. “A moment a truth, ain’t no way ’round it.” I shifted both bags of groceries to my left arm, and dug my right and into my pants pocket. I realized then, that at Elena’s suggestion I had changed my pants before we’d rushed off downtown. My knife was in the pocket of my other pants on the floor of the bedroom, or in the hamper in the bathroom. We reached the third floor and the door of our apartment and I could still hear what was following us. We went inside. I was aware of carefully placing the groceries on the kitchen table. Elena was saying something reasonable. Some remote double vision, different than the awareness of narrative while the thing itself is happening allowed me to imagine myself: first I heard the knocking on the door, the loud pounding, like a cop. I wasn’t going to search for my pants with the blade in the pocket. I went to the bookcase I had assembled of bricks and planks, grabbed a brick and went to the door. I knew I was going to smash his head in and the inevitability of it left me feeling refreshed and empty, like some protracted and futile labor had at last suddenly come to an end. I was surprised to hear the kitchen door bang against the wall, evidently I'd flung it open, and heard what must have been me screaming. He stood there, a lead pipe in the hand at his side. I knew the breath behind my ear. Elena's hands grabbled my right wrist, her weight hanging on my arm, her feet off the floor; I felt her swing like a bell, the brick in my hand above his skull. I turned to Elena first, to steady her on her feet. Heard crying. It wasn't Elena. The kid stood in the doorway weeping. Elena wouldn't let go. She tugged at my arm even though it was now at my side. "Let go," she said, "let." I hadn't meant to struggle with her, and soon as I realized I let the brick fall from my hand.

She asked the kid in. He just stood in the doorway swallowing the sound of his crying. I went to the cupboard and poured myself a shot. "Come," Elena was saying to the boy. I went back to the doorway, retrieved the brick, and returned it to its place as a support in my jerrybuilt bookcase. Elena led him in by the hand, shut the door, and sat him at the kitchen table. He sat there, dazed. I helped myself to a second shot. I began to see him more clearly. He looked about sixteen. The crying had stopped. His face was closed tight around some old hurt he was keeping secret from himself, and the world; the habitual anger barely held something terrible in check, rage a discipline that made his face cohere and hunched his shoulders. It was hard to believe that he had ever cried. He looked around the kitchen and through the archway to the living room, disoriented. He'd wound up in a weird place. On the wall was a canvas Elena had been working on that she was not ready to show, nor did she want to see it when she wasn't working on it. The work in progress was covered by a bed sheet. I thought the draped canvas was reminiscent of Jewish mourning practices. When one dies the grievers walk in stocking feet and shroud mirrors in white sheets. The kid looked at the large shrouded something, the radio had been left on and was playing one of Corelli's hits from the eighteenth century that must have sounded like a dirge to him. There were plants everywhere, strangely thriving. He appeared startled, had suffered an accident wherein he'd learned something he didn't want to know, self-knowledge an endless degradation, a tendency he preferred to hold in contempt. Elena served him a bowl of soup, placed a napkin and a spoon on the table. It was chicken soup, her mother's recipe, loaded with cilantro and other herbs and spices. Vapor curled up from the bowl. The boy, who Elena had addressed as Danny, sniffed at it cautiously. He didn't say a word. Elena, borrowing from a waiter in a restaurant on Second Avenue we went to from time to time—the waiter funny, extraordinarily rude, seemingly in conflict with his desire to nurture humanity while being a misanthrope, would answer a patron who asked what kind of soup had been placed before him (since the patron had not ordered it), and the waiter would say, "None of your business soup. Eat." When Elena said "None of your business soup,"

Danny didn't laugh. Demonstrating an explorer's courage, looking defiant, he tasted the soup. He wasn't a bad looking kid. His pale skin had a wind-lashed, reddish look and his eyes were too busy, reconnoitering. I wondered what he would have to face with his friends down in the stairwell. What would be incumbent on him now?

Overtime dwindled. I worked ten-hour days, but had the weekends. It was not quite dark when I got home, although the hallway kept its portion of night. There were evenings when there wasn't any sound from under the stairwell: Danny and his friends making forays, caught in skirmishes, or trying to cop drugs, scavenging, snatching purses.

Elena told me that midweek, after the incident at our doorway, Danny had stepped out of the dark, taken a bag of groceries out of her arm,s and carried it up to the apartment. He ignored the mix of hoots and applause from his friends.

Danny placed the groceries on the kitchen table. Elena said "Thank you," looked to her purse for a moment, considered tipping him, and decided against it. He saw and looked offended. Elena said, "I'm sorry." Danny accepted the invitation to a cup of coffee.

Danny's carrying the groceries for Elena became routine. I had my moments of paranoia. It occurred to me that he might be casing our apartment for a break-in, surveying what might be sold or pawned, and I wasn't comfortable with Elena being alone with him. She said not to worry, and I knew her assessment wasn't naïve, although I couldn't dispel my paranoia entirely. But it was true, as Elena reminded me, Danny and his pals did observe the unwritten law, their activities were confined to streets away from the home block.

I received a message from heaven. In the mailbox that wouldn't lock because it had been pried open too often, as were all the others in the vestibule—junkies from adjacent streets hunting for welfare checks that were easy to cash—in the mailbox with the bent lid was a manuscript I'd mailed out six months before and forgotten. This time the rejection slip contained a message. The editor said, "In spite of myself I've been engaged by the work. 'Chekhov Was A Doctor' has a wild untutored genius and although the story is not suitable for *Charon's Breath*, there are other magazines where it might find a home." I sat in the easy chair we had purchased from the Salvation Army and savored every syllable. Words of encouragement out of nowhere. Certainly the remark about my "wild, untutored genius" was an allusion to my apparent ignorance, all I still needed to learn. But the editor had felt compelled to communicate with me. I carried the rejection slip in my wallet, took it out and read it again and again. It felt like a reprieve, the infinite silence had vouchsafed me something. Elena and I had the weekend. She said that earlier that week her mother had come by and ran her hands over her now prominent belly, as if Señora Concepción were caressing a huge crystal ball, and announced, "Una neña," which would turn out to be true. As I sat in the peculiar wealth of the day, thinking about the daughter to come, I was moved to some impulse like casting bread upon the waters. If I extended kindness to the boy who carried groceries for my wife, maybe sometime a stranger in the world would help my child. The world could be terrible.

Elena was telling me about Danny. He had, after carrying packages for Elena several times, talked to her, said, "Yeah" and "thanks" when she offered coffee. Elena said he glanced around the apartment, not in preparation for burglary, but wondering what we had to conceal, as if this were the sum total of human ambition. From the kitchen he could see the bookshelves, the planks laid out on bricks stacked five feet high running the length of the wall. Elena thought he was impressed with the quantity of books, and he asked, "You read all those?" She said, "No, not all, it's um, like our eyes are bigger than our stomachs. If you'd like to borrow a book you can." He moved to a pile of textbooks stacked on the floor we hoped to sell back to the college bookstore. Elena said Danny thumbed through a biology text until he came across an illustration of a dinosaur that he held up to her. She asked if he'd seen the dinosaur bones at the Museum of Natural History; it was then that she learned, that except for a school trip to the museum when he was in the fourth grade, Danny rarely ventured out of the Bronx, almost never traveled beyond the neighborhoods that were his lair, and his stalking grounds.

Elena also learned that Danny lived with an elderly aunt; he never mentioned a mother or father and she knew better than to ask. He said that he'd quit school, taken out working papers when he was fourteen and worked for a while at a bowling alley and then at a supermarket. He said he was still bringing money home. Elena engaged his eyes but didn't ask how he was getting his money.

I cautioned Elena not to allow herself to become, somehow, Danny's social worker. She said "yes," she'd thought about that, but she also found herself thinking about what Danny would have to do to redeem himself in the eyes of his friends.

I was in some new place. At once humbled and exultant, the seeming ease of my readiness to kill happening in conjunction with a time I discovered myself truly married, knew I was happy, all of this happening in a fatigue that liberated my will so that my life was a surprise; perhaps it was this state of being that made it possible to dream and remember what I'd forgotten; now I could afford it.

Elena said she would have preferred to forget Danny, but she felt his life was in imminent danger. I knew also that Elena thought that however inadvertent, we bore some responsibility for Danny's predicament. She looked at me surmising her thoughts, surmised mine, and to provide some measure of hope said that she'd seen Danny in short sleeves and there weren't any track marks on his arms.

My experience in the army hadn't annulled what I would tell Danny. As I spoke I was aware that a year had passed since I had spoken to my brother this way, divulged and explored what might be true; because Morris who'd been diagnosed schizophrenic, and was frequently institutionalized, would appropriate what I related, and then when I visited him, he'd regale me with my life as his, so distorted and fantastic I couldn't bear it. When I visited Jacob my communication with him had become stilted, solicitous, and false, as my brother's acute and kindly gaze recognized. And talking to Danny, remembering again, I knew this shameful failure. When I'd told my brother I loved him it was only an aspiration, like loving humanity in the abstract, and Jacob had looked at me with unspeakable understanding.

Danny and I had been part of something intimate. I told him it started with Charlie Messina. I was fifteen, my kid brother was almost three years younger than me. Morris was playing marbles at the curb just a couple of houses down from our building. Charlie Messina, who was my age was sitting on the curb, near Morris, smoking a cigarette. I'm not sure what happened. Morris said later that he asked Charlie to move his feet, so he could aim his marble. Charlie ignored him, Morris repeated himself and Charlie smacked him. It all happened very quickly. I didn't see Morris getting hit, but when I turned I saw the blood running from Morris's nose, falling on his shirt in big blobs. Morris ran home, his head turned up to stem the flow, passed me as I ran toward Charlie Messina. I jumped into Charlie swinging, he fell and I went down on top of him. Charlie's head hit the pavement hard. When Mr. Stern, the druggist from across the street couldn't revive him, some neighbors hailed a cab and took Charlie to Greenpoint Hospital.

Charlie was back on the block by late afternoon with his head all bandaged up. It was then that I saw that if Charlie Messina noticed how much bigger he was than me I'd be in a lot of trouble. I was afraid, and when I saw Charlie I put on a ferocious face and he looked away.

My kid brother took to warning all kinds of people, "Better not bother me or I'm gonna get my brother after you." I begged him to stop. I explained, "Morris, you're going to get me in trouble with some bad people." But Morris just looked at me as though I was taking back a gift, ignoring the trust that we both knew I'd accepted long ago; and my quibbling interrupted the life he was dreaming as he parsed the events in my life suitably glorious to become his life. But my brother's blabbing my name up and down the street may have had nothing to do with Junior Cominski taking notice of me. It seems that the way I walked, my very existence was an offense to him. I knew of Junior. He was one of the neighborhood heavies. He was a couple of years ahead of me when we were in junior high. Junior Cominski had been placed in the CRMD class—that is Children of Retarded Mental Development. Junior and many in his class weren't retarded; they were among the most dangerous sociopaths lumped together with the mentally slow, or deranged, and all were kept in the school until they were sixteen and then turned loose.

The scraps I'd gotten into weren't unusual. I had made my place in the street and while I didn't strut I carried myself with easy pride. It may have been this, some presumption Junior felt I wasn't entitled to, something that cheapened his preeminence that he had to correct; the education meted out to me incidental to his imperative. I was an insult to him.

We all knew about his fight with Billy the Moose in the freight yard. He cut Billy, ripping him open from beneath his chest across his stomach. It was a miracle that Billy survived.

Of course, nobody yelled cop. When Junior went to the movies he never bought a ticket, he just walked in and the guy who collected the tickets looked at the floor and said nothing. Junior, like some other solitaries in the neighborhood wasn't in a gang; he was a law unto himself. The face he was born with, proof of the maker's malice; a drop of white stuff oozed from a droopy eye.

I was hanging out with my friends at the edge of an abandoned lot, littered with bags of garbage, piles of brick, assorted pieces of broken furniture, and a rotting mattress. It was early evening; almost everyone had gone home to supper. We three were always the ones who delayed going home to the last possible moment. Leo was assessing his chances of losing his virginity that weekend, when his cousin Lena came to visit. He said that a couple of months ago he'd given Lena a present at her sweet sixteen party, the recording of Georgia Gibbs singing "Kiss of Fire." He said that his older brother Vito claimed that Lena had let him go all the way. Leo wasn't certain he could trust his brother's claim, but he said, most of the time Vito told the truth, and if Lena could do it for Vito, she could do it for him too. Leo was seeking advice from me and Joey. I said I couldn't offer an opinion, I didn't know the girl. Joey wanted to return the discussion to the immortal achievements of Joe Dimaggio. Junior Cominski and Inch came strolling out of the lot. Cutting through a back alley and the lot was a short cut, a way of avoiding walking all around the block. I don't think Junior had been looking for me, but when he saw me he suddenly looked full of purpose. I could feel Leo and

Joey tense. Junior and Inch came up to us. Junior seemed to be thinking. There was something dismissive in his glance at Leo and Joey, but he required a sufficient presence for what he needed to demonstrate publicly. There was a principle at stake. I watched him think. Junior decided Joey and Leo would do and he grabbed my shirtfront. Inch stood at the ready. Inch Brody had been in the CRMD class with Junior. Inch was slow in learning, but devoted to Junior and assisted him in extortions and errands, whatever Junior commanded. Sometimes Junior would tell Inch to get lost; he tired of Inch trailing him like a shadow; and then Inch, who wasn't much taller than a fire hydrant, would wipe his constantly running nose and go off heartbroken. Bringing his face close to me, Junior said, "You think you're something." I didn't know whether to agree or disagree. Something in me pretended to be neutral, as though I were responding to a joke, and I was going to be a good sport about it. Junior was infuriated. Inch didn't understand but he looked concerned. Joey and Leo stood by, everything in their postures suggesting that they were bystanders obligated by protocol to remain there and be mindful. Junior shook me by my shirt front, "You think you're a hard guy?" Somebody with a rep and you can walk where you want? Who the fuck do you think you are?" My shoulders shrugged. Junior said, "Oh, you're a wise-ass too." I shook my head no, sincerely. "Show him Inch." Inch held out both his hands. In one hand Inch held a switchblade, in the other a zip gun. Junior said, "The zip ain't reliable, the fuckin' thing can blow up in your face, but it's what I got now. And the blade, which is good. If you think you're gonna duke it out with me you better wise up. Because if you pick up your hands I'm gonna fuckin' kill you, understan'?" And he shoved me, his fists pounded my chest. I stumbled back, couldn't lift my arms and fell. I sat in a pile of garbage. Junior said, "Next time I see you, you better cross the street, fuckin' disappear, or you ain't gonna go on breathin'."

Joey and Leo were mad at me; I'd made them see something they didn't want to see. My other friends heard about it, were embarrassed to be around me, and anyway, I preferred to be by myself. My brother was certain that I'd purposely failed him; he lingered at home, something fantastic brewing in his head. For a whole very long day I didn't wander out, not just because I was afraid, but in the street, I felt a scarlet letter burning on my brow. Finally sick of my fetid solitude I gave myself an airing. I went out through the basement, through a side door into the alley that opened into the lot filled with debris and garbage. The July sun heated the junk in the lot, the rank aroma the herald of summer, the warmth and stench welcome, a desultory haze I could walk in and not think.

The sunlight falling through the besotted air lit up a hunk of concrete out of which stood a pipe that looked like a cane. I moved toward it. The task claimed me, I didn't think why. Fat blue flies buzzed in the stinking scrim of air, falling like a swamp from heaven, I grasped the pipe anchored in the base of concrete and yanked. It may have been part of a plumbing fixture or a piece of a boiler system. The pipe extending upward was shaped like a cane and jeweled with rust; reddish-brown on the curving handle, yellowish-brown down the stem, and at the bottom, a nut with metallic mold, like the fossilized hoof of a bull rooted in concrete. I found another piece of pipe and began to whack away at the concrete base. Small pieces splintered away.

My hands hurt. I had to lay the pipe down for a while. I found a pile of bricks, and one at a time threw each brick hard as I could against the concrete base. After a time I weighted one foot on the concrete base, which seemed to me only a little smaller than when I started, grasped the rough-hewn pipe, pulled and yanked. I resumed banging and digging in the concrete with a piece of pipe I used as a hammer and a chisel. The palms of my hands blistered. Banging away, I lost my footing, fell and skinned my knee. I danced around the lot, cursed, and the pain ebbed into a low burn.

The swampish sky turned gray, what looked like night swallowed up midafternoon, it began to rain a steady drizzle.

I was soaked, whacking away blind, yanking and pulling at the iron cane, which may have been lead, and when it came free I stumbled backward but retained my footing.

I took it home, found a file at the bottom of a closet, near a hammer, a tin of shoe polish, and an enema bag. I filed and honed the cane. I wrapped thick black tape around the handle, filed and shaped the fist-sized hoof at the bottom.

When my mother saw me walking up and back in my bedroom with the cane she gasped, "Nu? He's practicing to be a cripple, he needs to bring down the kayn aynhoreh on our heads? Like we don't have enough tsuris!" When my father got home from work and sat down to supper she said to him, "You should see how your son spends his time." My father kept his nose close to his plate and chewed noisily. My brother's head swiveled from me to my father, to my mother, and back to me. "Gevalt!" Mother hollered, turning to me so that I could verify the phenomenon, "When that horse eats he's dead to the world!"

The next day I went walking with my cane. I didn't know what I would do if I encountered Junior. I was comforted by the cane, wanted to wield it, but didn't know if I'd be able. My body had become inert when Junior Cominski had brought his maniac's face close to mine and banged my chest, knocking me over into the pile of garbage. I didn't know that my body wouldn't become paralyzed again if I encountered him. But my feet carried me forward, zombie-like I wandered the neighborhood, even walking on his block, my guts rioting when I saw someone who turned out not to be Inch. I'd mistaken Tiny Harold schlepping a leg to his newspaper kiosk for Junior's shadow, Inch looming. Lame Harold arranged the piles of newspapers on the counter of his kiosk and fastened girlie magazines with clothespins to a wire overhead, in the kiosk's window opening. As I passed he nodded to me as if recognizing a kindred spirit. I made believe I didn't see him. I continued marching, fearful as the convicts I'd seen walking the last mile in the movies, ignorant of what I'd do when faced with Junior, not knowing if I could trust my body. I walked, in plain sight, hidden, dawdled in alleys among the cats slinking around garbage cans. I remembered Tiny Harold's lame shadow spilling over the pavement near my feet.

I did it the next day and the next. Word got around. I walked all week, pushing the odds, wondering if I'd accepted the possibility of death, questioned if I could rely on my arms to work when the time came—the weight of the cane in my hand giving me hope, the heft of it ballast I wouldn't want to squander.

I set off Saturday at about noon. Joey and Leo came out of the candy store across the street, laughed and called after me. I thought of how swiftly I'd attained untouchable status. "Hey you!" they called. I tapped the sidewalk with my cane, jaunty, as though I were a nonchalant boulevardier strolling into a day of sweet adventure. Joey and Leo laughed and called, "Wait up." I picked up my pace. They followed after me. I rested the cane on my shoulder, the pose of a man about to break into a tap dance, and walked faster. They began to trot after me, pausing when laughter doubled them up. I couldn't run away, but I had nothing I wanted to say to them.

"Ay yo-Davey," Joey said, using my name as though nothing had happened. "Jeezus" Leo said, "You don't wanna hurt nobody." Joey said, "Maybe he does," and then the two doubled up again, laughing. I started to walk away. "For Chris' sake, hold on a fuckin' minute, you don't know," and they were again overcome with laughter. Joey racked with laughter, tears squeezed from his eyes, said, "It's sad really, I guess …" and surrendered to the hilarity of it all.

They told me, keeping a distance. I hadn't shed my defiled status, nevertheless they were compelled; what had happened belonged to me in some way, and I should know it all: what they were about to say was even funnier than my fate and they couldn't resist telling me.

Junior Cominski and Inch had gone into Berman's Bakery. There wasn't anything unusual about this. They did it often, each eating a cupcake they didn't pay for and leaving. On the evening Junior had dumped me into the pile of garbage, they had gone to the bakery. Junior ate a cupcake, and then a jelly donut, and half of a cheesecake. Inch smiled and did what Junior did. He ate a cupcake, a jelly donut, and the other half of the cheesecake. When old Mr. Berman was about to protest, Junior said, "Shut the fuck up." Inch pointed his finger at Mr. Berman as Junior had when he gave warning.

Judy, Mr. Berman's unmarried daughter, in the back of the bakery telephoned Mr. Facetti. Mr. Berman like all the shopkeepers in the neighborhood paid a protection fee to Mr. Facetti's representative. Mr. Berman, never a man to stir up trouble, would never have called Mr. Facetti direct, but might have passed on the matter to his representative.

Joey and Leo said nobody laid a finger on Inch; he couldn't be held responsible. And probably if Junior hadn't got loud with Mr. Facetti's people he wouldn't have got hurt. "Maybe," Joey said, "Junior was stupid as well as nuts." "Junior never had no self control," said Leo.

It may have been an accident. The enforcer was pissed off and got carried away. The beating Junior took left him simpler than Inch. Leo and Joey heard that Junior was sent to a place that was sort of a hospital, where the staff would see if Junior could learn to dress himself, things like that.

Inch was inconsolable. He wandered the neighborhood like one blind at birth, suddenly afflicted with sight, he couldn't make sense of what the light brought to his eyes. Bewildered and walking in circles at a street corner, he waited for someone to help him cross the street. One of Mr. Facetti's people arranged for Inch to help out Yudi Bloom the bookmaker. Eventually Inch recovered, forgot Junior, and ran errands for Yudi.

"So," Danny said, "You punked out." "Yeah?" I said, the inflection in my voice making it a question. Danny said, "Chicken," not allowing that there could be anything more to it. Elena brought apples, cheese, and bread to the table. I got myself a can of beer from the refrigerator, hesitated, and then thought what the hell, and gave Danny one. He smiled and said "Thanks." I tried to explain to Danny and myself what I thought was true. Junior and Inch had become part of my submerged history and to obliterate my moment of cowardice I'd committed countless reckless acts, put my life at risk over and over to annul an event even after I'd forgotten it, as the smell of being a pariah launched me from one rooftop to another, me clinging to the back of speeding buses—and I found myself in confrontations and brawls I had no right to survive.

I sipped my beer. I thought, Danny like Elena had been

raised Catholic. I entered into a simile and lost my way, struggled, not sure how much I'd said out loud: see, like a calculus of Hail Marys and Our Fathers for venal and mortal sins, I had no idea how many reckless or brave acts were necessary. And Elena had heard it too, the story that had kept itself secret from me. My face was burning.

Then I saw, or thought I saw, that my hackneyed sincerity had embarrassed us both. Danny looked away. What I'd admitted in front of my wife wasn't so much truth telling as self-indulgence. And who was I to presume this avuncular role with him anyway. Danny thanked me for the beer. I began to doubt what I'd said. There was silence. When it was clear that I wasn't going to offer him another beer, he got up, ready to leave. Elena and I were surprised when Danny lingered at the door and said, apropos of I don't know what, that he'd wanted to be a fireman. He said he had an uncle in the department who had once offered to help. But, Danny said, he'd have to get his high school equivalency to have a shot at it. Elena offered to help. Danny said, "I don't know," and "good night." Later I wondered if Danny and his friends were involved with any of the insurance fires incinerating the South Bronx, or the fires set for fun.

I poured myself a nightcap. Elena frowned and got ready for bed. The drink warmed me; despite all I'd said, finally I blurted to Elena what I hadn't been able to say, "Danny boy, I thought if we told the truth our souls might be priests to one another." Elena said, "Come to bed."

We lay quiet for a long time. Elena moved her head from

the pillow to my shoulder, "Someday you'll have to be able to say such things without the help of a drink, or you'll lose me." I said, "Yes, I know." She didn't comment on the Junior Cominski saga and I was grateful. Elena sat up. "Davey, I've never met your brother. You've told me about him, but I've never met him. You don't want me to meet him?" "Sure, yes, of course, you can meet him. We can go on Sunday if you like. He's living in a supervised group home in Queens. He's a sweet man; I think you'll like him, almost everyone does."

I telephoned and made arrangements for the visit. Sunday the weather was fine. I awoke cranky. Then I remembered with relief that the interminable argument I'd had with my father was a dream I'd had just before waking. In the dream I would finally lose all sense of language, croaking sounds that lacked even animal meaning. Awake, sipping coffee, I continued to justify myself, grateful for the coherent arithmetic, as if my father were present, I calculated the shylock's vigorish that would take three years of his life, the price of the mink coat my father had purchased for the love of my life.

Morris's room was an ample size, set up as an efficiency apartment; he had his own bathroom and shared a communal kitchen. The place was orderly and clean. He'd made changes since the last time I visited, mitigating the motel room feel of the place with some of his own furniture: a battered but attractive easy chair, a bookcase packed with his books, a plaid bedspread, a goldfish bowl on the dresser with two goldfish, and a parakeet perched on a swing inside its open cage. On the wall was a framed Mary Cassatt print, a mother bathing a child. Morris and I looked at one another and laughed; the present a continuation of the absurdity we'd always known. We might have been kids again, on our way to the Saturday matinee, ready to plunge into the semi-dark bedlam of the theatre, ready to immerse ourselves and believe narratives as unbelievable, but less threatening than the one we were living, and it was unbearably funny.

Elena and Morris hit it off right away, talking about Mary Cassatt. Morris and I hugged; it felt good. I said, "You're going to be an uncle." He applauded, his eyes lit up, he hesitated, and hugged Elena; she returned the embrace. They talked about Mary Cassatt and her paintings of mothers and children. The discussion led Morris to talk about our childhood, our parents, and the old neighborhood. He said our parents had been children when they had us, "Hard pressed children." "Mom," he said, "wasn't quite sixteen when you were born; Pop was what? Seventeen?" I nodded yes. Everything Morris said seemed to have the humane distance of a sociologist whose understanding made benevolence possible. I began to wonder and hope, again. I'd read of cases where schizophrenics, after years, inexplicably emerged from delusion. The psychiatrists ventured theories as to why. Could it be? Morris growing out of his illness, like some protracted childhood sickness that had finally burned itself out. This good fortune coincident with the present enrichment of my life, Elena, and the child to come.

Elena and Morris talked. Elena was charmed. Morris said, "I'm in love with your wife." Then he was quiet. Elena said, "It's okay." Morris said, "I have to ask you a favor." I said, "Yes." Elena said, "Sure." Morris didn't say anything else. I said, "Please, what?" He said, "Really?" I said, "Of course." Morris said, "Chinese food. There's a great takeout place just two blocks away. I can chip in, there's money on the dresser." "It's our treat." "Great," Morris said, "please, spare ribs and sweet and sour shrimp."

As we headed for the subway Elena asked, "Can we afford a cab? My feet are killing me." I said, "Yeah sure." We waited at the corner. Many cabs went by, they all had passengers. At last one pulled up to the curb. I bent my head to the window, told the cabbie our destination, and he said, "I'm off duty," and sped away. Elena said, "Next time don't tell the cabby where we're going until we get into the cab."

We waited. Elena said, "Your brother has the most open face I've ever seen on a grownup." "Yes?" I said, "sometimes it's a liability." "I imagine. Davey?" "Yes." "Well, while you were out getting the food he told me about his experiences in Korea. I began to wonder which one of you was crazy. Morris described carrying this old Korean man on his back, up and down mountains, trying to find medical care for the old man's wounded foot. Your brother said that the old man was a kind of guru, and it was only the wise old man's counsel that enabled Morris to complete his journey. Morris said he had to make his way through minefields and artillery barrages hauling the sage on his back. He began to tremble. He struggled to stifle his crying. The trauma made him lose control of his bladder. I wanted to help; he was suffering, really. He rushed to the bathroom, cleaned himself up, and changed his pants. When you got back he was calm again." "Morris," I said, "was almost thirteen during the Korean War." Elena said, "Yes, I know." And then as I flagged down an approaching cab, Elena said, "Maybe there's a kind of wild justice in it." "Justice? What the hell are you talking about?" "Well, your brother appropriates pieces of your life for his story, and you take what you need from people for your stories. Only Morris's fictions are rampant, totalitarian."

We settled ourselves in the cab and told the driver our address. He looked at very pregnant Elena with alarm. She said, "Don't worry I'm not going to have a baby in your cab. Just take us home." The cab shot off and we bounced in our seats.

I got home from work a little later than usual. At first I thought I'd walked into the wrong building. The tenements on either side of the one l lived in were identical. There were fluorescent lights overhead illuminating a freshly painted banana yellow hallway. Not a sound from under the stairwell. The various radios and babble from behind the apartment doors flowed into a sedate din. I was about to leave when I saw El Super, spattered with paint, at the far end of the vestibule; he was carrying a ladder and muttering something in Spanish. When he saw me he said, "Terrible, terrible, solembambitches, it's in the papers." Standing under the stark fluorescent light in the freshly painted hall, tired at the end of the long day, and looking forward to my supper, I sensed some connection between general catastrophe, the new terrible light, and the painting of the vestibule. I nodded greeting to El Super and climbed up the stairs. As I trudged up I was spooked by the feeling that I was going to be a father in an age that would require wisdom.

Elena stood in the center of the living room holding her stomach with both hands, wincing, her eyes were red and puffy. The rush that heated my head and peeled my eyes took in a print Elena had pinned to the wall I hadn't seen before; and I was shouting, "Get your coat, we're going to the hospital." Elena shook her head "no." I yelled at her. She said, "It's only our daughter, dancing in there." And I thought, I'll have to argue patiently, if it hurts enough to make her cry we should go to the hospital. Before I said another word, she said, "It isn't necessary, really." She waddled to the kitchen and placed on the table a plate of rice and beans, and what was more unusual, a bottle of beer. I looked more closely at the print Elena had tacked to the wall. She had begun to transfer the composition in broad abstract lines to a canvas propped on her easel. The print, one I'd never seen before, was Carpaccio's "Meditation on The Passion." On a marble slab lay the dead body of Christ, all human color leached out of it, his bone-white face empty of everything except the fossilized grimace of pain. Standing in the forefront, a lean sage in a loincloth who looked like he might have dined on locusts, but never honey, raised one reasoning finger toward heaven, reverential and stupefied in the desert. I knew it was too soon to ask Elena questions about her new project. I suggested she get off her feet and rest; I didn't need to be waited on. And she told me—Danny and three of his friends were arrested. There had been a turf war: two kids had been killed, one a bystander, and the other, according to the newspaper account, deliberately shot by Danny Ryan, "assassinated." A witness had testified that Danny had put a second shot into the wounded boy.

I was at work the first time Mr. Dugan the social worker knocked at our door. Elena said she'd asked him in and served tea. He sat at the kitchen table, stared at the cup of tea until it got cold and said that his workload now included over a hundred cases. Elena commiserated and he said that he visited Danny in jail. Elena emptied Mr. Dugan's cup into the sink, poured hot tea into the cup, and set it in front of him. Mr. Dugan said, "Thanks" and went on to say that because Danny was a minor he would be sent to reformatory, but given Danny's troubled relationship with authority, now that he was caught up in the penal system there was a very real chance he'd never get out; and he might get himself killed while inside. Mr. Dugan placed his hand over his heart and said he'd never lost track of Danny, it was only that the last couple of months he'd been very busy and Danny had been elusive. Elena said she'd tried to be sympathetic to Mr. Dugan, but he was waiting for absolution and she couldn't say anything more. Then Mr. Dugan said that Danny had asked if he could write to us; Danny hoped we'd answer his letters.

Mr. Dugan visited again two evenings later and delivered the same message. Bald Mr. Dugan, carrying a brief case, in a suit and a tie, needed a shave. He might have been forty or sixty years old. Solemn and weary he begged for crucial information, the relevance of which he'd forgotten. Elena asked about Danny's aunt. Mr. Dugan said she was very old and could not live on her own, and he was working on that problem. I lied and said "Okay, I'll write to Danny." Mr. Dugan repeated that Danny was ashamed of his handwriting and spelling; the fact that he'd asked for this correspondence could be a positive step. I imagined years of letters, Danny in our lives as he grew into a schooled psychopath. And I thought, as Mr. Dugan drank the tea that had grown tepid, and Elena laboriously raised herself out of a kitchen chair, I thought that Danny's bullshit detector had been working when I talked to him. For all I'd said, he could see that my life had been animated in the moment I found myself free to kill him, anything I said afterward was only conversation. As Mr. Dugan got ready to leave he looked at Elena's drawings tacked to the wall and the half-finished painting on the easel, and asked "Who's the artist?" I said, "She is," as Elena struggled to her feet. I heard a trickle, looked at the small puddle gathering between Elena's feet. Elena looked, laughed and said, "My water broke." Mr. Dugan ran ahead and had a cab waiting for us at the curb.

SAUL AND DAVEY

My soul ladles out sleep. The snoring I hear is not me, it is my wife, and I laugh because the sound is the only unbeautiful thing about her, and I would share the joke with my father but it is happening in a future that doesn't yet exist. My old man loosens the arm clamped around my neck, and with the other he gestures toward the crowd and explains, "I wanna buy him a pair of shoes." Someone is yelling, "Call the cops." Pop has me in a headlock; bent over at the waist I stare at the pavement. If I stretch my neck I can breathe and see the crowd that has gathered. I'm a veteran, in uniform, twenty-years old, and my father is strangling me. I struggle. My arms are around his waist. I attempt a bear hug, bending him backward to break his grip, but the old man is still too strong for me.

So there we are, in front of the shoe store, locked together, Saul and Davey, like a hunk of erotic Hindu sculpture. His free hand clamps his chest, trembles, as though to keep the wild dog of his heart from jumping out of his ribs and running loose in the streets. He yells, "Why should he deny me? I'm his father, no?" The frowning woman with the headless pullet sticking out of her shopping bag nods and says, "Ingrates, every one of them." From somewhere at the center of the crowd an old woman's voice quavers, "My Arnold is a prince." "Look," Pop says, searching the crowd for the voice that said "My Arnold is a Prince," "I'm asking so much? I want to buy him shoes." The little bald guy standing next to the woman with the shopping bag studies my face. "Mr.," he says, "the boy is turning colors—now blue!" "Davey you alright?" Pop asks and loosens his hold. My ears are burning. I straighten up, rub my neck, and view the avenue. There are many stores. I want to go to the shops and shed my uniform, peel khaki for civilian garb. I have a pocket full of money. Pop surveys me, head to toe. "Please," he says, "let me buy you the shoes, nice, sporty, two-toned." His hand gestures to the window full of shining shoes, "Florsheim," he says. "Listen," I say, returning us to the argument just before we got to the shoe store, "Roosevelt carried out Socialism on a stretcher." "Oh yeah," he says, "I know what's eatin' you, and you're just changin' the subject, Stalin was right to knock off Trotsky, see? That Leon was a pain in the ass intellectual." So just as I was about to say in the kitchen, before Korea, when Momma interrupted to hug and say goodbye and the dialectics had reached the point where it would wreck the furniture, I remind the old man that he had been a sucker for Roosevelt. "Sucker" I say. "Whatta you mean?" says Pop, his eyes gone glassy wet, face red. I jab the naked place. "Franklin Delano Roosevelt" I spit out, naming my old man's bimbo. "Oh yeah," he says, "Oh yeah," slipping his hand inside his shirt, fingering the laces of his truss. "Yeah," I say, "what did Roosevelt do for working people, but throw them a few crumbs?—he saved his own kind, the millionaires." "Whatta you know about it, sonny boy?" "I know that the world still belongs to the people who make money from money, or maybe you got a depreciation allowance for your back?" "Listen to him," Pop says, "your mother's womb was your soup kitchen, sonny. You got rosy and chubby floatin' around in there, she went down to eighty pounds, she was all tits and eyes." So now he's gonna beat me over the head with that. Momma's flesh and blood, my bread and wine, "Whatta you want me to do? Living things are expensive." "So yeah," he says, smiling, "so let me at least get you the shoes."

Up and down the avenue as the shoppers move from store to store, some stop at the spectacle of us and join in the argument. I can hear from the loaded windows stacked to the sky, and all the voices of the jammed avenue a bawling, peripatetic harangue. Parents and children, wives and husbands, grandparents, everyone accusing and screaming. Car horns blare and honk. A small pickup truck goes by filling the air with the smell of herring. The letters on the side of the truck read, "Barney Greengrass the Sturgeon King." A merchant is cranking an iron handle, rolling up an awning that shades a window display. The store sells umbrellas, handbags, various accessories and lightweight folding chairs. I want to buy my mother one of the folding chairs. Momma loves the sun, illicitly. On occasion, on a bright warm day she allows herself a moment of standing by the kitchen window; thinking, no doubt, that the manmade world is a place unfit for children. I dream of the grave Jewish Madonna, indulging herself, seated in the folding chair in front of her building, basking in the sun. And I must find a suitable gift for my brother. There is a luggage store where I can buy a suitcase to replace my duffel bag, stuffed with underwear, and books, which I've stored in a locker at Port Authority.

Pop is heating up again, and I know he'd mangle me, right here, if it weren't for his sense of the larger betrayal, the injustice at the heart of all. The labor theory of value does not apply to love. The most costly things cannot be earned. "So," he says, "you still doin' that writin'?" " I'm trying to learn." "Tryin' to learn? You gonna spend your life bein' anudder unborn genius?" "I'm here," I insist. "For cryin' out loud, be a mensch. You got a mouth, you got words, fine, you could be a labor lawyer, do something real for people." A breeze makes Pop's receding white hair stand on end. I say, "What about Steinbeck?" "What about him?" "He wrote the *Grapes of Wrath* and Congress passed laws to help the migrant workers." "All right,"

Pop says, "You just proved my point, you can open a mouth." "And Zola," I say, "he wasn't an enemy either, think what he did for Dreyfus." My father looks weary. "Okay wise guy, while you're scribblin', how you goin' to eat? What are you gonna do for a livin'?" "I'm thinking of maybe going back to school, becoming a teacher." "A teacher," he sighs, "okay, you're too nervous to steal." "Momma is waiting," I remind him, "and I havc to get out of my soldier suit. She'll be happier to see me in civilian clothes." He says, "All right. But don't be an anti-Semite"—which he pronounces "antuh—suh-mit," his accusation a warning that I'm in danger of the ultimate misanthropy—an antuh-suh-mit. "At least let me get you the shoes. Wait here, I know your size."

Pop rushes into Florsheim's. His broad back fills the doorway. I take off. I'm running. I've got a good lead on him, at least a block. I speed by people who look disapprovingly at me. I hear them shouting encouragement in my father's direction. I know they're pointing at my back as I turn the corner. I look over my shoulder and he is nowhere in sight. I look again, and there he is. He's coming on, he won't quit the chase. Tucked under his arm, like a football, is the box of shoes. I think I can outrun him.

Courting Laura Providencia
A novel by Jack Pulaski

Fifteen years in the writing, the novel bursts forth with a cast of characters that are sometimes warm and familiar, and at other times violently distorted as in a funhouse mirror. *Courting Laura Providencia* is a literary devotional; a rumba of this American life; a tale of love and the occasional fall or return to redemption.

"In his smart and sure-footed new novel, set in New York City after World War II, Jack Pulaski tells two interlocking stories ... both a version of the age-old story of lovers from two clans and a brightly colored record of a complex community in Brooklyn."

THE NEW YORK TIMES BOOK REVIEW

Paper 0-939010-67-4 $14.95 438 pages
Cloth 0-939010-68-2 $27.00

The St. Veronica Gig Stories
Short stories by Jack Pulaski

Set in the immigrant streets and tenements of Brooklyn, Jack Pulaski's stories sparkle with incident, character, memory, and a touch of the surreal. In "Religious Instruction," a widowed scripture teacher channels her passion into a retelling of the primal stories of the Bible that transfixes her adolescent students: "When she marries again we will not hear these stories, not the same way." "Music Story" sketches a chilling portrait of urban ethnic territoriality, while in "Father of the Bride," a young Jew pursues the skeptical, profane and eccentric Carlos, seeking his daughter's hand.

"Get the book and read it. And then shower copies on everyone you know who still enjoys moving his or her eyes from left to right."

SVEN BIRKERTS

Paper 0-939010-09-7 $8.95 170 pages
Cloth 0-939010-68-2 $15.95